TIME WILL TELL

CHANTAL FERNANDO

CHANTAL FERNANDO
Published February 2015
Cover design © Arijana Karčić, Cover It! Designs
Edited by Hot Tree Editing

ISBN-13: 978-1506143071
ISBN-10: 1506143075

DEDICATION

For Stephanie Knowles
Thank you for all that you do!

PROLOGUE

XANDER

My father is dead.

Jack Kane was one of the most important people in my life, and now he is gone. I am walking around like a normal person, but I feel anything but normal. I'm just going through the motions of life. I'm not living. I'm just not dying. There is a difference. I feel like part of me is missing, as if my spine were ripped and pulled out of me, and now I'm left to try to manage whatever I have left.

My dad is everything to me.

Was everything.

It has been a month.

How can he be gone?

Jack Kane was a strong man; nothing was supposed to be able to touch him, right?

That's what I always thought growing up. He was formidable; nothing would faze my dad. He was the man I wanted to be growing up. He wasn't perfect, but I never expected him to be. And he didn't expect me to be a perfect son either, and God knows I wasn't.

I was a terror.

But he loved me unconditionally, and he was there for me no matter what.

I can't believe this has happened. I always thought my dad was invincible.

Surely, a man like him wouldn't walk home from a night drinking at the bar, only to be hit by a man who *had* been drinking, but made the stupid, selfish decision to get in the car and drive, right?

The irony wasn't lost on me.

I stare at the front door, willing him to open it and walk in. The house is empty, filled with memories, taunting me, reminding me of how things once were.

It's a bittersweet feeling.

It somehow makes me even lonelier.

Just one more time. If only I could see him one more time. What would I say to him? That I was proud? Knew I was lucky to have him as a father? That I was sorry for being a wild kid, making his life hard at times?

I wipe my cheek when I feel something wet slide down it.

I can't remember the last time I cried. I think it was when I was just a boy. I'm glad no one is around to see me like this—so fuckin' weak. After putting all my energy and focus into comforting my sister, Summer, I'm now able to focus on myself. While my sister was close to my dad, she didn't see him much growing up. She'd only really been in his life for the last few years due to her crazy-ass controlling mother. Me, on the other hand, I've been close to my dad since the day I opened my eyes.

He was my hero.

He was rough around the edges, hung around with bikers, and drank and swore a lot. But he was tough and had a heart of gold.

Now he is six feet under.

I stand and pace the hallway, running my fingers through my hair and tugging on the ends.

And then I make a decision.
For the first time in my life, I just need to leave.
To get away. Be somewhere else.
I need to be free.
Does time heal all wounds?
I guess only time will tell.

CHAPTER ONE

TRILLIAN

I stare down at the cake in appreciation. I think it's my finest creation yet—chocolate on vanilla, circular in shape, and covered in chocolate candy. The cake is for my best friend and partner in crime, April. It's her twenty-first birthday today, so here I am at nine in the morning, finishing off the cake I'm going to surprise her with, although it won't really be a surprise. I bake cakes for everyone I know. I write 'Happy 21st Birthday April' on the bottom front of the cake in pink icing to top it off.

Perfect.

She's going to love it.

My phone beeps with a message from her. Speak of the devil.

April: I love you.

I smile widely and message back.

Trill: I see you got my present.

April: It just came to the door! Seriously? You spoil me! Thank you. I love it.

I'd gotten her Ed Sheeran concert tickets and a chocolate bouquet delivered to her house.

Trill: Glad you like it.

April: Be at my place at six. Can't wait for tonight!

I'm meeting April at her house for dinner, cake, and drinks before heading out for a night of dancing and, what would you know, more drinking. I'm not much of a drinker really. I hardly go out partying except for occasions like these, where April is involved and I can hardly say no. I'm a little on the boring side, at least that's what I'm told. I'd rather be snuggled up with a good book than out shaking my arse on the dance floor, but that's just me.

April is the complete opposite of me. She loves to go out and try different things. She pulls me out of my comfort zone, which I don't always like but know that I need.

I'm in my last year of university, studying to be a kindergarten teacher, and I bake cakes or read in my spare time. That doesn't sound like the description of an average twenty-one-year-old girl, but it's me.

What can I say, I'm a creature of habit. Every morning, seven a.m. on the dot, I like to run. In addition to helping me keep in shape, running also gives me a chance to clear my head. I have a good life, but it isn't perfect. My mother left me with my dad when I was seven years old and I haven't seen her since. Apparently, being a mother and wife of a trucker wasn't all that she had thought it would be.

When my dad died two years ago from cancer, I was left alone. I do have family scattered around the country, but none of them live close to where I live, and I don't really want to move. My house belonged to my father and he loved it. I couldn't bear to sell it or leave it. My dad worked hard to pay as much as he could on the house, so the mortgage is extremely low. And thanks to Dad's insurance policy he left for me, I was able to pay it off completely. Between selling cakes, working part time at an ice-cream parlour, and the money in my bank from the insurance payout, I'm doing okay. Pretty well, even. But I'd trade it all just for one more day with him.

Grabbing one of the extra cupcakes I made last night for my neighbour, Zach, I take a bite and slowly walk into my room. Today is Friday and I have two classes to attend before I can come back home and worry about what to wear tonight to April's.

A knock at the front door has me stopping to change directions. Licking the icing from my fingers, I open the door with my right hand.

"Is that one of my cupcakes?" Zach asks, eyes narrowing on my fingers.

I smirk, then bring the cupcake to my mouth and finish the last bite. "So what if it is?"

Zach grins as he pushes the door open and walks inside, heading straight to the kitchen. I close the front door and follow behind him. "You only made twelve!"

I laugh. "You're so damn spoiled, Zach. Are twelve cupcakes not enough for you?"

He picks up one and takes a huge bite, half of the cupcake disappearing into his mouth. "Yeah, if it was only me eating them. Every fucker comes and takes one."

He places some money on the table and I look at him in disapproval. "Don't start with me."

"Just shut up and take the money, Trill," he says, licking icing from his mouth.

"You know I don't charge family," I say quietly.

And Zach was the closest thing to family that I had.

He and his dad have lived next door for the last four years. Zach and I became friends, and the two of them had kept an eye on me ever since my dad passed away. An extremely unlikely friendship, considering Zach's dad, Grim, is the president of the Wind Dragons Motorcycle Club. Zach is my age and also in the MC. I call him the biker prince whenever I want to piss him off. He's wearing his cut right now, on top of a tight white t-shirt and worn jeans. He's an attractive man with reddish brown hair and clear pale blue eyes. When I'd first met him, I'd had a little crush on him. But our relationship soon changed into one of friendship and I couldn't even think of him any other way.

"I know you don't expect me to pay, Trill, but I want to," he says. "April's birthday thing tonight, yea?"

I nod. "Yeah, you going to come out?"

He rubs his hand through his messy hair. "I'll be around. Gotta keep an eye on you, after all."

I scowl. "I can look after myself."

He chuckles and pats me on top of my head. Like a dog. "You have no street smarts, babe. You're a good little innocent girl."

I flip him off. "Just because you don't see me twerking every weekend doesn't mean I don't have street smarts."

Zach starts laughing. Hard.

My lips tighten. "You're picturing me twerking, aren't you?"

He slaps at his thigh. "Yes, I am, and it's fucking hilarious."

"Hey, I'm a decent dancer!" I say, offended.

"You're a good dancer. Well, I've only seen you dance once at your birthday. But I didn't see you shaking your ass or looking like you were fucking someone on the dance floor."

My eyes widen. "Who dances like they're fucking?"

Okay, maybe I've seen that in video clips, but never anything that bad in a club.

"Women in general," he replies, smirking. "Trust me."

"Maybe they act that way around you," I say, my eyebrows furrowing. "I've seen how stupid women get around you."

He flexes his biceps. "I have my charms."

I roll my eyes. "You *think* you have your charms."

He scoffs, eyes dancing with amusement. "I think you're the only woman in town who's immune."

"That's because I'm the only woman in town who knows the real you," I fire back, proud of my wit.

He puts his palm over his heart. "Innocent little Trillian, my ass. You have a sharp tongue."

I laugh, my shoulders shaking. "You're the one who calls me innocent. I've never referred to myself like that."

He pulls me into him and kisses me sloppily on my cheek. I push him away and quickly wipe my cheek. "Zach!"

"You love me."

"You're okay," I mutter.

"Every time I leave this house I feel like my ego is that much smaller," he grumbles.

I shake my head, fighting a smile. "Then my work here is done."

Zach is easy to be around—at least he is with me. I saw another side of him once, but I have a feeling that side comes out more often when he's with his club.

"Remember I told you about my friend Xander?" he asks as he takes an apple out of my fruit bowl and takes a bite.

"Yeah, I remember," I say. "Your childhood friend. You guys see each other once a year, don't you?"

He nods, chewing slowly. "We try to, yeah."

We live in a town called Channon. It's a country town and about a ten-hour drive from the city.

"So what about him?" I ask, curious.

"He rang me and asked if it was okay if he came to stay for a couple of days."

I smile. "You must be happy about that."

"I am," he says, swallowing then taking another bite of the apple. "We always have good times. I'm worried about him, though. He just lost his dad. You remember I went to a funeral last month? For Jack Kane?"

I bob my head. "I remember."

"Jack was Xander's dad."

I swallow hard, my expression softening. "I'm sorry to hear that. Maybe he wants to come here and clear his head, get away for a while."

I know firsthand how much losing a parent hurts. I'd never wish it on my worst enemy.

If I had a worst enemy.

He sighs and picks up the box of cupcakes in one hand, half his apple still held in the other. "Yeah, it looks like it. It fucking sucks. I know how close they were. It'll be good to see him, despite the circumstances. Anyway, I'll see you tonight, Trill. Lock the door after me."

"Okay," I reply, locking the door as he leaves. I clean up the kitchen then have a shower and get dressed for uni.

CHAPTER TWO

TRILLIAN

"This cake is amazing," April says as she takes another huge bite.

"I'm glad you like it."

"Like it? I fucking love it. You should open your own shop," she says, moaning.

My lip twitches as I watch her devouring the cake and making orgasm noises. "So I've been told."

"Trill, you look stunning tonight!" Amanda calls out. All April's closest friends are here. Some I know, like Amanda, and some I don't.

"Thank you, Amanda, so do you," I say shyly, fiddling with the hem of my black dress. It isn't anything too revealing, nothing like what April is wearing, but it's fitted and shows my figure. I'm not a slender girl. I'm curvy with an hourglass shape, or so April tells me. I have wide hips, a bigger ass than I'd like, and my breasts are more than a handful.

"Told you," April says. "Love your hair like that, too."

My hair is normally extremely curly, but tonight, I've tamed it with a hair iron and it's dead straight, sleek, and falling down my back. "Thank you."

"Do you want another drink?" she asks, eyeing the premade vodka mixed drink I'm holding.

It's a girly drink.

It also doesn't have too much alcohol in it, and I don't mind the taste, mainly because you can't taste any of the alcohol.

"I'm good," I tell her.

She reaches up and plays with a lock of my hair. "I wish I had your hair."

I eye her slim body, blonde hair and wide blue eyes. "Shut up, April."

She laughs, and then takes a sip of her drink. "I'm serious, Trill. It's so black it almost looks blue, and with your bright blue eyes, holy hell."

I look down into my drink, trying to hide my blush. "Thanks, girl."

"Hey, just being honest. You okay here? I'm going to mingle."

"Go ahead," I tell her, smiling. "You don't need to babysit me."

She puts her hand on her hip. "I know. I just know this really isn't your scene so I like to keep a close eye on you."

I roll my eyes. "I'm fine. I'm enjoying my drink and listening to the music."

She nods. "I'll just check in with everyone and be back."

She walks off, her hips swaying as she talks with some of her other friends. I finish my drink then get up and head to the fridge for another one. I choose a cranberry and vodka this time, then smirk to myself—look at me, trying new things.

"Hey, Trill," Amanda says from behind me. "Guess what I heard today?"

This doesn't sound good. "What?"

"Richard is coming to Drake's tonight."

Drake's is one of the pubs in town we're going to tonight. April works there on the weekends as a bartender, sometimes even on weekdays after school. She's studying to be a teacher, like me, but high school instead of primary.

"And?"

"And he told me he wanted to ask you out," she says, grinning. "Come on. He's good looking, admit it."

He's okay. I mean there's nothing wrong with him. I just don't feel any kind of attraction between the two of us. It explains why he comes to get ice cream almost every shift I work. My hours every week are the same and he usually seems to pop up.

"I'm not interested, but I'm sure he's a nice guy," I say. "Why don't you go for him?"

She grins. "Maybe. I am looking for someone to party with tonight."

"Well, there you go," I say with a smile.

Two birds with one stone.

"If only Zach would even look my way," she mutters, tipping back her drink.

"Zach will be there, too, probably," I say to her.

"Yeah, but he's not interested," she pouts. "He's so dreamy. I don't know how you live next to him without jumping his bones every night."

I choke on my drink. "I manage."

We all hang out for the next hour before we pile into two maxi taxis and head to the pub. The place is packed when we get there, pretty usual for a Friday night. I start to regret wearing four inch heels as we line up to enter. With a stamp on each of our wrists, we walk inside as one big group, but soon split up as some of the girls head for the bar and some for the dance floor. April and I choose the dance floor. I try to let loose as much as I can, swaying to the music.

A few songs later, I tap April on the shoulder. "I'm going to get some water. Do you want some?"

She shakes her head and flashes me a smile that I return. I head to the bar then open my handbag and take out my wallet. When I look up to my right, I do a double take.

Wow.

I've definitely never seen this man before. I'd never forget that chiselled face, shoulder length light brown hair, hazel eyes, a strong jaw, and lips I wouldn't mind sucking on. He is beautiful and I'm intrigued. I've never felt an instant attraction like this before in my life, and I don't know how to react. Sucking in a shallow breath, I look straight ahead of me. Okay, I need another look. Trying to be as inconspicuous as possible, I tilt my head slightly to raise my gaze to his to find him already looking in my direction.

Busted.

"Hi," he says, lips kicking up at each corner.

He has a sexy smile, too.

I look around, making sure he's talking to me.

He is.

Shit. He is.

I scan his features once more.

He's good-looking.

No, he's more than that. He's fucking good-looking.

Delicious.

Amazing.

Wow.

How long have I been staring?

My gaze lowers to his full lips, currently curled up on each side with a cute dimple in his chin. Both of his arms are covered in tattoos, two full sleeves, and I can see some peeking out from his black t-shirt.

"Hi," I reply, pushing my hair back behind my ear. I avert my eyes and look straight ahead, trying to get the bartender's attention.

"Are you here with someone?" he asks in that deep tone of his, scanning the bar before bringing his gaze back to me.

"My friends," I reply, cheeks flushing slightly under his penetrating stare.

"What's your name—"

"Hey, sexy," a woman purrs as she slides up next to him.

He turns his head and smiles at her, but it looks forced. "Hello."

"Would you like to dance?" she asks, licking her lips invitingly.

He shakes his head, turning to look at me for a second before returning to her. "No, thank you."

"Are you sure?" she asks, batting her eyelashes. "Maybe you could give me your number and I can call you some other time?"

"Sorry," he replies, rubbing the back of his neck. "I'm not interested."

It's an embarrassing thing to watch, someone being rejected, but I can't seem to look away.

She turns from him, glares at me, and then walks away. What the hell did I do?

"Can I get you a drink?" he asks, making me glance at him again.

"Thanks, but it's okay," I reply, smiling. "What's your name?"

"Sexy, apparently," he muses, his lip twitching.

Well, the woman wasn't wrong.

"Are you just stopping through town?" I ask, curious about him.

He nods. "That obvious, huh?"

I'd never seen him around before, so I'd taken a guess. I order a bottle of water and pay for it myself.

"Stubborn," I hear him mutter under his breath.

My eyebrows arch. "Because I don't want a stranger buying me a drink?"

His lips twitch. "Okay, if it was anyone other than me offering, I'd say it was smart."

"Are you the exception to every rule then?"

"You said it, not me," he replies with a smirk.

April walks up behind me and wraps her arms around my waist. "Trillian, who the hell is this delicious man?"

The man in question smiles at April, and then looks back at me. "Trillian," he says slowly, as if testing it on his tongue. "Beautiful."

April digs her fingers into me. "Holy shit."

I glare at her, which she painfully ignores.

"Do you want to dance, Trillian?"

I swallow hard. Do I want to dance?

He holds his hand out and I take it without thinking. April is always telling me I need to be more spontaneous, to let go every once in a while, to take a few chances every now and again. Why not start now? He leads me to the centre of the dance floor. He boldly puts his hands on my waist and pulls me flush against him.

"Is this where they've been hiding all the beautiful women?" he says in my ear, making goose bumps appear on my arms.

"There are lots of beautiful women in Channon," I say, looking around.

I'm nervous. I don't do too well with new people and someone like him is way out of my comfort zone. However, for some reason, I don't want to leave.

He shakes his head as if I've missed his meaning and pulls me closer to him. Moving his body in rhythm to the music, his eyes never leave mine. Of course, he's a good dancer, too. I look down shyly as I sway my hips. A finger lifts my chin back up. "You have no idea how stunning you are, do you?"

Is that a rhetorical question?

I don't know.

Not knowing where to look, my eyes touch on everything around me until I have no option, but to glance up at him. Each time, his eyes are on me, a heated expression on his face.

He looks like he wants to eat me alive, and I don't know what to do with it. All I know is it exhilarates me. Blood is pumping through my body, my pulse racing, and my palms are sweaty.

I don't think I've ever been so unnerved around a member of the opposite sex. What is it about him? I'm drawn to him and it's more than his good looks. I've met many good-looking men in my life, but none of them looked at me like he is. None of them studied me with such intensity, like they wanted to know everything about me. Like they were taking the time to figure me out, wanting to see inside my soul.

Maybe I'm just losing my damn mind.

Our bodies touch for the entire song, and when it ends, he reluctantly takes a step back, puts his hand on my back, and walks with me back to the bar. His fingers scorch my lower back, burning into my skin. I'm so attuned to him that I can almost feel his every movement.

"Trill, we're going to the next bar," April says, touching my arm, but her eyes are not on me.

"Where are you going?" he asks her, stepping even closer to me. I can feel the heat from his body and fight the urge to sink into him.

"Dream. Why, are you coming?" she asks him boldly, arching an eyebrow.

He holds my hand and smiles. "I am. But I'll bring Trillian with me."

He will?

I shoot him a look for making decisions for me, but he only grins in response, looking amused.

"Have you been drinking?" April asks, glancing at him in suspicion.

He shakes his head. "One drink. I'm fine. I wouldn't put Trillian in danger."

April glances at me and smiles. "Your call, Trill. Are you going to meet us there?"

Am I?

I don't reply.

April pulls me aside and says, "He's drop dead gorgeous and can't take his eyes off you. Live a little! I'll see you at Dream."

I roll my eyes. She doesn't need to give me her usual speech because the words are already playing in my head.

She walks off and I stare after her, trying to remind myself why exactly I am friends with her.

"You can go with them if you want," the sexy stranger says, looking a little disappointed. His hazel eyes dart from me to April, who is on her way out of the club.

"I want to go with you," I say, realising it's the truth.

Why not, right? It's just a ride to the next bar. Dream isn't far away, and maybe I'll get to learn more about this mysterious man.

His slow spreading smile could light up the entire street. "Good," he murmurs, lifting his hand and placing it on the side of my neck. "Do you want to go now?"

I nod. "Sure."

Side by side, we walk outside to the car park, our arms touching. When he stops in front of an angry-looking black matte bike, my mouth drops open.

"Never been on a bike before?" he asks, sounding like he already knows the answer to that.

I shake my head and play with the strap of my handbag. "Never."

He tilts his head toward his bike. "It will be fun. Come on."

I take two steps toward his bike, and then stop. "I don't know…"

"Come on, live a little, Trill."

He heard April's words.

And are we on a nickname basis, now? I don't even know his name. I asked once, didn't get an answer, and now am shy about asking again. I'll find out eventually.

He puts his hands on my waist, and my heart races.

"Please," he says, watching me.

How the hell am I supposed to say no?

"Okay," I say, blowing out a breath. "Sure, why not."

I can do this.

If I die, I'll make sure to haunt him.

He smiles widely, takes my hand in his, and walks me to the bike. Grabbing the helmet, he puts it on my head and fixes it for me. "I like your hair. It's beautiful."

Why does this suddenly feel like a date?

It isn't one.

I need to remember that.

"Thank you," I reply quietly.

"Don't thank me, it's the truth."

He takes off his jacket and hands it to me. "Put it on or you'll freeze."

I slide my arms into his leather jacket one by one then close the front. He reaches down and zips it up for me. "It's huge on you, but it will have to do."

It isn't *that* big on me, but it's nice of him to say it.

He straddles the bike, and then turns to me, holding out his hand. "You ready?"

I nod, accept his hand, and get on behind him. He reaches behind and takes my hands in each of his, wrapping them around his waist to rest on his abs.

And boy, does he have abs. His stomach is hard as a damn rock.

"Hold on tight," he says before he starts up the engine. I held on for dear life, scowling when I feel him laughing, his body shaking with the effort. I lay my cheek against his warm back and close my eyes, enjoying the feel of him.

As he rides down the road, I open my eyes and look around.

I feel the wind on my face.

I like it.

I feel free.

I like that, too.

A smile appears on my face.

I don't want this ride to end.

*****

The bike comes to a stop in the Dream car park.

I slide off, my legs a little shaky, take the helmet off, and hand it back to him.

"What did you think?" he asks after he gets off the bike and stands next to me, watching me.

I look down and then back up at him. "I fucking loved it."

He smiles widely, his eyes lighting up. "I knew you would."

"I'm serious, it felt amazing. So free. I was scared at first, but then I really enjoyed it," I say, trying to explain the emotions I went through. I take off his jacket and hand it back to him. "Thank you."

His eyes soften on me as he takes the jacket from my hands, our fingers touching. "My pleasure."

We walk into the bar.

"I'm going to go see April," I tell him, needing to be away from him for a moment. What the hell am I doing? Going on motorbike rides with strangers? This isn't like me. I haven't done anything like this in my life.

I don't know if that's sad or not, but it sounds like it.

It's also safe.

I'm usually safe.

Predictable.

I'm the type of girl who would probably meet her future husband on an online dating site where they match up your compatibility instead of putting herself out there and meeting new people.

Tonight is unusual for me. And all I've done is dance with a gorgeous man and then take a ride with him.

Why the hell am I complaining again?

I got here safely and experienced my first ride on a motorcycle, which I fucking loved in the end.

I want to do it again and again.

April sees me and her eyes light up. "You made it! What are you doing here? If it were me, I'd be anywhere—fucking the shit out of that guy!"

I roll my eyes at that. "He's around here."

She smiles and pulls me in for a dance. A few songs later, I tell her I want to get some water from the bar and walk away from the dance floor. I glance around for *him*, but I don't see him anywhere.

When I see Zach at the bar, I head straight for him and take a seat next to him. "What's a girl gotta do to get a man to buy her a drink around here?"

His head snaps to me, his eyes roaming down from my face to what he can see of my body. "Look at you, Trill. You look beautiful."

"Thank you. You don't look so bad yourself."

"Water?" he asks.

"Yes, please."

"Can I get a bottle of water?" he asks the bartender when he passes us. "You been drinking?" he asks, studying me.

I shrug. "I had two drinks."

The bartender slides over a bottle of water and Zach hands it over to me. I crack open the lid and take a long drink. I didn't realise how thirsty I was.

"You having a good night?" he asks.

I put the bottle of water down on the table and nod. "I am. It actually feels good to get out."

I'm surprised by my comment. I have genuinely enjoyed tonight, and I had a good time.

"Good, you deserve it."

"I only had two girly drinks. I don't think I could handle what April was drinking."

He leans down and cups my face. "Such a good little responsible girl."

"Hey, Zach, there you are." A familiar deep voice comes from behind me.

Zach lets me go and laughs. "Trill, this is Xander. Xander, this is Trillian."

I turn and stare into a pair of deep hazel eyes.

Well, shit.

Xander? Zach's friend Xander, who's staying with him for a couple of days?

I hate small towns.

"We've already met," he says, gaze wandering over my face curiously.

"You have?" Zach asks his hand now on my nape.

Xander nods. "I went to Drake's but just missed you. She was there."

Zach glances down at me. "Right, how was Drake's?"

"It was good. Packed as usual," I answer, but my eyes are on Xander, who is looking everywhere but at me.

"Not surprised. I left after about fifteen minutes."

"You didn't mention that you had a woman," Xander says after he orders himself a drink. He sounds angry.

Wait, he thinks I'm Zach's girlfriend? Why the hell would I have danced with him then?

Zach wraps an arm around me and kisses the top of my head. "That's 'cause she's not my woman."

Confusion flashes over Xander's face before he is able to mask it. "She's not?"

"Nope," Zach replies. "She's Trillian."

Xander looks even more confused after that comment.

"Where's the birthday girl?" Zach asks.

"On the dance floor," I reply, pointing to where April is dancing with Amanda and Molly, a friend she works with.

"Looks like she's enjoying herself," he says. "You coming home with me, tonight?"

I'm watching Xander when Zach asks me that, and I don't understand his expression. He looks… angry?

"Yeah, may as well," I tell Zach, looking back to him. "What time will you be leaving?"

"Whenever you're ready to go is fine," he says, downs his drink, and then stands up. "I'm going to go and wish April happy birthday. Xander, keep an eye on Trill for me, will you?"

Xander nods and sits down next to me. I watch Zach hug April and pull her in for a dance.

"That doesn't bother you?" Xander asks in a deep rumble, watching the same spot I am looking.

"Why would it?" I ask, turning to look at him.

Hazel eyes framed by thick, dark lashes meet mine. "I feel like I'm missing something here."

My lip twitches. "Why do you say that?"

He licks his bottom lip. "Never mind. It doesn't matter."

"You get in today?" I ask, knowing that he did. Zach didn't mention this morning that he was arriving today, just that he was going to arrive.

He nods. "Yeah, I rode in a couple of hours ago."

"You must be tired," I say, playing with the label on my bottle of water.

He shrugs his broad shoulders. "I can sleep tomorrow. Zach really wanted to go out, and now I guess I know why."

I'm confused. "Why?"

He looks down at my dress and clears his throat. "You never mentioned you knew Zach."

"Neither did you," I say, staring at his profile before turning away.

"Small town," he mutters, shifting in his seat. "I should have known."

Is he bored? Maybe he wants to dance with someone else. Shit, I'm horrible at making small talk, and I have no idea what to say. All I know is that I don't want him to stop talking to me.

"Thanks for the ride here," I say.

He turns to me, eyes softening slightly. "You're welcome. I'm surprised you haven't been on a bike before, seeing as you're close with Zach."

I shrug sheepishly. "He's tried before, but I always told him no."

His gaze turns intense at that, his eyes searching mine. He wants an explanation as to why I let him, a stranger, when I wouldn't let Zach, someone he can obviously see I'm close to. I don't have an answer either, so he isn't going to get one.

"Why did you go with me then?" he asks, his brows furrowing.

"I don't know," I say. "I guess I decided it was now or never."

I can't explain it.

"I'm sorry, by the way," I blurt out. "About your dad."

Real smooth, Trillian. Reaaalll smooth.

He looks my way. "Zach told you about that, huh."

I glance down at my hands. "I'm sorry. I shouldn't have brought it up. Especially, when you're out trying to have a good night."

"It's all right," he says. "And thank you."

"If there's anything I can do…" I trail off, even though I don't think there is. I don't think he'll want to talk to a stranger about how he's feeling, and I don't think baking him something will help.

Shit.

Maybe I should just stop talking.

CHAPTER THREE

XANDER

Anything she can do to help?

Images of her lying out bare before me flash through my head.

Fuck, she is a beauty.

A natural beauty.

Midnight black, thick, long hair that I want to run my hands through. Clear, porcelain skin, and wide blue eyes that stare back at you like she can see into your soul. A pouty red mouth that I want to taste and a lush, curvy figure that I wouldn't mind exploring.

She's also off limits.

Just my fucking luck.

When I saw her standing at the bar tonight, I was drawn to her. She has a rare natural beauty to her, a much-understated beauty. I knew I had to talk to her. And she's sweet—soft-spoken, kind and sweet. Every time she blushed, I wanted to push her against the closest wall and have my way with her. Taste her sweetness. Keep it for only me. I don't remember ever being so instantly attracted to a woman in my life.

And she's connected to Zach somehow, which changes things.

Although he said she wasn't his woman, his actions say differently. He also asked her if she is going home with him tonight, and she said yes without hesitation. Are they just casual fuck buddies? For some reason, I don't like that. This girl, Trillian, deserves more.

Trillian.

An unusual name, but it suits her. It's pretty and unique.

Fuck, am I going to start writing poetry or some shit soon?

Why did she dance with me, take a ride with me? Especially if she'd never been on the back of a bike before. I don't understand this girl. Sure, we didn't kiss or anything like that. Technically, we didn't do anything friends wouldn't do, but it felt like more. She doesn't know me, but she took a chance on me, she trusted me. She wanted to be around me, let me take her around.

Zach stared at her with adoration and genuine affection in his eyes, like he worships the ground she walks on. And he should. A short time in her presence and I can tell that her beauty isn't only skin deep. She's a woman that, if you get her, you keep her. A good woman. Wife material.

She obviously has something to do with Zach, so I'm not going to go there. I'm not going to stay here for long, so it isn't like I have anything to offer her other than a casual fuck or two.

"How old are you?" I ask her.

"Twenty-two," she replies out of that sensual mouth of hers.

Twenty-two, she's the same age as Zach and me. Yet she seems younger somehow.

Innocent.

"Have you lived in Channon your whole life?" I find myself asking.

She nods, looking down at her hands again. "Born and bred."

"Are you happy here?"

She glances up and smiles. "I am. I love it here, although I would like to travel at some point."

"You haven't been anywhere?" I ask, my eyes widening.

She grins. "I've been around Australia, yes, and I've been to Bali. That's it."

I chew on a piece of ice from my whiskey as she continues, "I'm still young. I have time."

She finishes the last of the water and places the bottle on the bar.

"Do you want me to get you another bottle?" I ask her.

"No," she says. "But thank you, Xander. You're very sweet, you know that?"

I shrug like it's no big deal, but really, I like hearing it.

I was so fucked.

"I don't know about that," I mumble.

She puts her hand on my shoulder. "I hope we can hang out a bit before you go. I could show you around town if Zach is busy."

I wonder if she knows Zach is a biker. She has to know. She's lived in this town her whole life, so she obviously knows who the Wind Dragons MC is.

"I'd like that," I tell her.

If Zach doesn't have a problem with it, of course.

I see Grim, Zach's dad, walking up to us.

"Xander," he says, slapping me on the back. "Good to see you, son."

"Good to be here, Grim," I say, staring into the eyes of one of my dad's very best friends. Grim is a good man and a tough leader of the Wind Dragons MC. He's one person you don't want to cross, but at the same time if he likes you, he is fiercely loyal and a good friend to have in your corner. He looks down at Trillian and smiles. "Look at you, darlin', you look pretty. Anyone I need to beat the shit out of for not keeping their hands to themselves?"

Trillian laughs and I hang on to the sound. "No, I'm good, but thanks, Grim."

Grim smiles back and nods. "Where's that son of mine?"

"Out on the dance floor," I tell him.

Grim sighs. "When does that boy ever have his dick in his pants?"

I couldn't be sure, but I thought I heard Trillian mumble, "Whenever he's at my house."

I am fucking confused. Is Trillian with him or not?

Grim glances at me, then at Trillian, then back at me.

"Trill's a good girl," he suddenly says, eyes narrowing.

I nod. "I know."

Message received.

"Good," he replies. "I'll see you around, Xander. Bye, Trill, darling. Get home safe, you hear me?"

"I will. Bye, Grim," Trillian says, her eyes going back to the dance floor.

I turn away from her, my eyes scanning the crowd. Zach is dancing with some other girl now, but Trillian doesn't seem to mind. Maybe they have an open relationship. Zach hasn't mentioned anyone named Trillian before. Maybe it's a new thing.

Either way, I'm not getting a taste of her. It isn't happening, so I need to stop thinking about it. I didn't come here for this, to start something with someone. I came here to try to sort myself out, to work on a few things. To learn how to deal with being here without my dad. The last thing I need is to be hung up on a girl that I can't have and don't deserve.

Zach returns with a girl walking behind him. "Xander, this is…"

He looks down at the girl.

"Paulina," she says.

"Paulina, right, I knew that," he says, looking amused. "Paulina, why don't you show my buddy Xander here a good time?"

She's pretty enough with a nice figure and blonde hair. Her red lips are from a tube, not natural colour like Trillian has. She sits on my lap and rubs herself against me. I glance at Trillian to see her stand up, say something to Zach, and then head for the dance floor. Zach follows her, but not before sending a smirk my way.

I ignore the pang of regret that I feel as she walks away from me.

I don't get to have everything I want, and I know that.

"Fuck, you're gorgeous," she purrs in my ear. "Do you want to leave?"

Do I want to leave?

I glance over and watch Zach pull Trillian in for a dance.

Yeah, I want to leave.

With Trillian.

But that isn't happening.

Paula—*is that her name?*—licks the shell of my ear and I think, why not?

I have nothing to lose and a night of pleasure is just what I need.

It's been a while—about two months. That might not be long for some, but it is for me.

"Come home with me," she purrs once more. "Trust me, you won't regret it. No won't be in my vocabulary tonight."

My eyes widen at that.

I stand and allow her to lead me out.

Do I have condoms in my wallet? I'm pretty sure I have two. That's going to have to do for tonight because there is no way in hell I'm going to take her without any protection. If she's this easy for me, she's likely this easy for others. Not a nice thing to say, but it's the truth.

We get into a taxi because I didn't want to take her on my bike. I can pick it up tomorrow.

She gives me head on the way home.

Classy, I know, but I'm not complaining.

I come in her mouth, wishing it were another.

Fuck, how has she gotten to me after only meeting her once?

It's stupid.

I push her out of my mind and allow myself to enjoy the rest of the night. Uncomplicated, meaningless, dirty sex.

That's just what I need.

CHAPTER FOUR

TRILLIAN

After Xander had left last night, I stayed and tried to enjoy the rest of the night. I danced with Zach and April, and two hours later, Zach and I dropped a drunk April off at her house before going back to ours. He didn't mention Xander and neither did I. He walked me to my door as he usually does and waited for me to get inside safely before heading to his own house.

This morning, I woke up later than I was supposed to. I pressed snooze four times on my alarm, then had a shower and got dressed quickly for work. Walking out my door, a cup of coffee in my hand, already five minutes late for work, I rush to my car. This is definitely a first. I know my boss won't be mad at me for that reason alone, but still, I hate to be late for anything. I place the cup of coffee on top of my car as I unlock the doors. When a taxi stops in front of Zach's house and I see Xander slide out, I quickly look away. My chest tightens to the point of pain. I don't know why it hurts so much that he spent the night with that woman.

Disappointment—that's what I'm feeling.

Pure, utter disappointment.

He obviously isn't attracted to me in that way and I have to accept that. Unable to stop myself, I glance up to see his eyes on me. I see him grimace slightly, caught doing the walk of shame.

Is it even called that for a man?

Not wanting it to be awkward, I force myself to say something. "Hey, Xander."

It isn't his fault that he doesn't want me. We can be friends. I can keep the fact that I am attracted to him more than I've ever been attracted to anyone before in my life to myself.

"Hey, Trillian," he says in that husky voice of his. He stares at my house and then looks back at me. "You live next door?"

I nod. "I do. Didn't Zach mention that?"

He scowls. "No, no, he didn't. He's spoken about his neighbour before, but I didn't realise it was you."

"Oh," I say. "Well, yeah, that's me. Anyway, I'll see you around. I hope you had fun last night."

I cringe, covering my face with my hair, using it as a shield.

Yes, I just said that.

Kill me now.

I get into my car and pull out of the driveway, only to see Xander standing there watching me. Forcing myself to look away, I turn right onto the road. I have to get to work. I don't have time to think about Xander and what he was up to last night. It doesn't even matter anymore. So I have a little crush on him, big deal. It isn't like I'm in love with him. I just met him, for Christ's sake.

When I arrive at work, I realise that I left the coffee on top of my car and drove away with it.

No wonder Xander was staring.

He must think I'm a complete idiot.

Cringing, I cover my face with my hands for a second before getting a wet cloth from work to wipe the coffee from my car. Then, with a heavy sigh, I walk back into Candy Creamery to start my shift.

*****

I'm about to clock out when Richard walks in. I remember what Amanda said about him coming out last night, but I didn't see him.

"Hey, Richard, what can I get you?" I ask politely.

"The usual, please," he says, smiling. "I was hoping to see you last night, but apparently, I just missed you."

Well, that explains it.

I scoop up some chocolate ice cream and put it in a wafer cone. "Yeah, it was a good night."

Richard shifts on his feet. "Are you seeing anyone, Trillian?"

I hand him the cone and bite my bottom lip. How do you explain to someone that no, you aren't seeing anyone, but you also aren't interested, without hurting their feelings? There is nothing wrong with Richard, and I'm sure he would make a woman very lucky, but that woman isn't going to be me.

"No, I'm not," I mumble, taking the ten-dollar note from his hand as he reaches out with it.

"Are you free next weekend? I thought maybe I could…" He trails off and I lift my eyes from the cash register to see Zach walking in. He stands next to Richard.

"Trill, gimme some ice cream," Zach says, grinning.

I shake my head.

He's standing here, dressed in all black, wearing his cut, demanding ice cream like a little kid.

"Wait your turn, Zach," I tell him, giving Richard back his change, and then offering him an apologetic smile.

"I guess I'll talk to you next time," Richard says. "Have a good day, Trillian."

Zach eyes him as he leaves, waiting for him to exit before he speaks. "He wants you. Bad."

"He was about to ask me out," I admit.

Zach smirks. "Like he has a chance."

I make him a cookies and cream cone. "And why would you say that? He's good looking and nice enough."

He shrugs and puts his hands in his pockets. "Not your type."

I roll my eyes. "I don't have a type."

I don't have much experience with men. I may not be a virgin, but I haven't had that much sex, either.

"So, what brings you here? I'm surprised you're even out of bed."

I hand him the ice cream cone and put my hand out for the money.

Zach grins and hands me a twenty. "I actually need a favour."

"Of course you do," I mutter. "What do you need?"

"I got some club shit going on tonight, so I was wondering if maybe you could keep Xander company?" he asks.

I hand him his change and think about how to answer this. Zach knows I would have no plans tonight, but I don't want to be alone with Xander. Not only do I turn into a bumbling idiot, but after last night and this morning, it's going to be extremely awkward.

"Can't he hang out with that chick from last night?" I ask. He did sleep with her, after all. Surely, he would be more comfortable around her.

Zach chuckles. "She was an easy lay. He's not going to see her again."

It's a small town, but I don't bother to point that out. I still run into Cain, the guy I lost my virginity to at seventeen. Yeah, not so good times.

"I saw him coming in this morning," I say. "He didn't even know I lived next door."

Zack licks his ice cream, then answers. "I know, he asked me why I didn't tell him."

"Why didn't you?" I ask, curious.

He shrugs. "I saw him staring at you last night. I didn't want him to make you feel awkward. I know how you get. You freeze up, then try to think of an excuse to turn the guy down without hurting him, but end up saying yes last minute anyway."

Do I do that?

I think back to Richard only moments ago. Would I have given in and said yes just to avoid hurting his feelings?

Maybe.

Shit, I am a pushover.

"And what if I was interested?" I ask, staring Zach straight in the eye.

"In Xander?" he asks with his mouth dropping open.

"If you repeat this conversation, I will kill you in your sleep," I growl, leaning over the counter.

Zach rubs the back of his neck with his free hand. "Fuck, Trill. He's just passing through, and you aren't a casual kind of girl."

I'm really not. But I've also never wanted someone the way I want Xander. I sigh and lean on my elbows. "It doesn't matter. Fine, I'll hang out with Xander tonight."

"Wait a minute, you wanted Xander? And then I set him up with that…" he trails off, scowling.

"It's fine," I say. "I just thought he was good-looking. No big deal." I try to play it off.

"Why didn't you say something, Trill? Shit, I've brought so many of my brothers around you and you didn't even bat an eyelash. How was I supposed to know who would catch your interest?"

I stand up straight. "Doesn't matter."

Zach is still staring at me, wide-eyed. "In the years I've known you, you've never, ever, even fuckin' once admitted to liking someone even a little bit. It does matter."

I decide to be blunt. "Like you said, he's just passing through and he's already found someone to keep him busy while he's here, so please, just forget we ever had this conversation."

"Fine," he mumbles. "Now I feel like shit."

"Well, don't," I reply. "I'm obviously not his type anyway, and that's okay."

I'm his *Richard*, if that makes sense.

"What the fuck do you mean, you're his Richard? Are you crazy?" Zach snaps at me.

Shit, I didn't mean to say that out loud.

My boss decides to walk in at that moment. She smiles at Zach and tells me I can clock out. Zach follows me to my car, muttering under his breath the whole way. I unlock the door and open it.

"See you at home."

"Trill—"

I turn to him. "Please don't embarrass me with this."

"Fine," he says, holding the door open for me to slide in. Before he shuts it, he leans down and says quietly, "You deserve the best, you know that, right?"

I puff out a breath. "See you later, Zach."

He closes the door and I drive home.

CHAPTER FIVE

XANDER

"If you're busy tonight, that's cool. I didn't expect you to drop your life when I came here," I tell Zach, who is playing a video game.

"I have some shit at the clubhouse I need to be there for, but Trillian said she would come over and take you out somewhere," he replies, staring at the screen.

I clear my throat. I had wanted to ask more about her all day, but was waiting for an opening. "So the two of you never hooked up?" I ask.

Zach pauses the game and turns to me. "No, we don't see each other like that. We're good friends. Family even."

I run my teeth along my bottom lip. "It's just that last night, I thought she was yours. I know you said she wasn't, so I thought it was casual or something."

"She's not casual," he replies, a thoughtful expression on his face. "As long as I've known her, I've never seen or heard of her hooking up with anyone. She gets asked out, maybe even goes on a date or two, but that's about it."

"My mistake," I reply.

My huge fucking mistake.

She isn't going to look twice at me now.

"You like her, don't you?" Zach asks.

I look away. "She's beautiful, of course…"

"Why didn't you fucking say something last night?" he growls, looking angry.

I sit up straighter. "When was I going to say something? When you were all over her? Or when your dad was giving me threatening looks and telling me how she's such a good girl?"

Zach cringes. "I wasn't all over her, and yeah, Dad's protective, but he'll get over it."

"You were all over her." And I didn't fucking like it.

"Why the fuck would you go home with that girl if you liked Trillian? That's fuckin' stupid."

I look at my friend, and for the first time since we were kids, I want to strangle the shit out of him. "I thought you and she had a thing, your dad silently threatened me, and I'm just passing through and have nothing to offer except a quick fuck. Pick one, Zachary."

"Shit, no need to full name me," he mutters.

"Why does it seem like you want me to hook up with Trill?" I ask, suspicious.

He resumes the game and continues to play. "You're a good man, Xander. She could do a lot worse."

Well, this good man left with another woman last night and ruined his chances.

"Thanks, I think. Not that it matters now."

Zach flashes me an odd look. "I guess not. Do you want her number? Or will you just go next door?"

"Are you sure she wants to hang out with me?" I ask. Maybe she doesn't even care that I left with Paula last night. Zach said she didn't usually pay attention to any men. Why the hell would I be any different?

"Yeah, she said she would."

Either she doesn't care or the woman is a saint.

"I'll just go over to her house then, I guess. Will her parents be there or what?" I ask, wondering what her parents will think of her hanging out with me. Then again, she hangs out with Zach, and I'm not any worse than he is. Unless they have a problem with tattoos, then I'm shit out of luck.

Zach's body goes still. "She lives there alone. Why do you think I check on her all the time?"

"What do you mean, she lives there alone?" I ask, scowling.

A young, beautiful, sweet girl like her living alone? I don't like it.

"Her dad died two years back," Zach replies in a low tone.

"Shit."

Looks like we have something fucked up in common.

"Yeah, now she's alone."

"Her mum?" I ask, hoping she isn't dead, too.

"Left her when she was a kid. No one knows where she is," Zach replies sadly, turning off the game and staring straight ahead of him.

"That's fucked up," I say quietly.

"Yeah, no idea how she came out so well. But her dad was awesome, loved her to bits. She was devastated when he died."

That sounds familiar.

"And now she has no one?" I ask, feeling for the beautiful girl. She is way too young to have lost both her parents and to be living all alone. I've lost my dad, but I still have my mum and sister. She has no one, and here I am feeling sorry for myself when she has it a million times worse. I think about what it must have been like for her, my chest starting to hurt.

Does she do everything for herself with no help? How does she manage financially?

Fuck, she's such an independent, strong girl.

Zach throws me a look. "She has me, dickhead."

I really don't think that makes up for the loss of her family, but I decide to change the subject. "Where's Grim, anyway?"

"He stays at the clubhouse more often than not. It's usually just me here. I'd probably be there more often, too if it weren't for Trillian."

So much for changing the subject.

"Dad's got some club business tonight. He's meeting with Sin, the president of another chapter of Wind Dragons."

Sounded like club shit that I didn't need to know.

"I could just stay in tonight," I think aloud.

Zach shrugs. "Then she can keep you company for a bit. I already spoke to her about it. If you want, I'll go over to her place and say you don't feel like going out. She'll probably assume you have other plans like—"

"I'll go," I interrupt. "It's a Saturday night. There should be shit to do, right?"

Zach chuckles, knowing he has me. "Sure. The usual nightlife, movies, parties and all that shit."

"What do you have going on at the clubhouse?" I ask curiously, lifting my feet up onto the coffee table in front of me.

"Party," he replies, grinning. "I'd bring you, but it's for Wind Dragon club members only. Like I said, another chapter is here and we always show them a good time. Offer them our hospitality and shit."

"I can only imagine what kind of party," I reply in a dry tone, making Zach laugh.

"You could always prospect for the club and find out," he says, smirking. Not the first time he's said something like this, and it won't be the last.

"No, thanks," I reply. "This is just a temporary visit."

"I know, I know," he mutters. "Did you enjoy last night?"

I glance at him. "I don't kiss and tell."

More like, I don't fuck and tell because I actually didn't kiss her on the mouth. I know that makes me an asshole, but she knew why she was there and it wasn't for me to romance her with sweet kisses—it was for both of us to get off. Besides, after staring at Trillian's lips all night, hers paled in comparison, and I had no desire to taste them.

"Well, I know from experience, she's good at head," he adds casually.

Did he really just say that? This guy.

My eyes narrow dangerously. "Please don't tell me you passed me your sloppy seconds?"

He shrugs. "What? It's hard to find a hot girl in town I haven't been with."

You could look right next door for one.

"You're something else, you know that?" I reply, shaking my head. "We're close but we're not that close. I don't want someone who's had your dick in her mouth."

Zach laughs, spreading his arms out on the back of the couch. "It was a while back, don't worry. It wasn't like it happened recently."

That's not the fucking the point.

"The next time you bring a girl my way, I'm going to be a lot more wary." As in, I'm going to say no way in hell.

"Oh, come on, I was a good host."

I shake my head at him. "You're fuckin' insane."

He just grins.

Why is he my friend again?

I knock on the door twice and take a step back. Rubbing my palms together, I hear the door unlock then slide open.

"Hey, Xander," she says, smiling shyly. Her cheeks are a little pink, and her hair is tied up and piled on top of her head. She's so beautiful that for a second, I don't speak, but just take her in.

"Xander?"

"Hey, Trillian," I finally say.

She opens the door wider. "Come on in, make yourself at home."

I step inside and she closes the door behind me. I smell something delicious and sweet.

"What did you want to do tonight?" she asks as we walk side by side into a large kitchen. She stands next to the oven while I stare at her ass as she bends over to open it.

"What would you normally be doing tonight?" I ask, wanting to know more about her.

She straightens and turns to me. "Nothing much. Studying, probably. Or reading. Or baking."

I glance down at the oven. "What are you baking?"

She grins and I notice a dimple in her right cheek. Christ, she's fuckin' cute.

"Cupcakes. Have a seat."

I move to the table and take a seat.

"Can I get you something to drink or eat?" she asks as she watches me.

Fuck, she's sweet.

"I'm okay, thanks. I thought we could maybe grab some dinner somewhere," I say. I haven't eaten anything since Zach and I had pizza for lunch.

"Okay, sounds good," she replies. "I'll just finish the cupcakes and then we can go."

I nod. I want to address what happened last night, but know there isn't a way to speak about it without the two of us admitting what is going on in our heads. I don't think I'm ready for that, and I have no idea how she feels. She's just a gorgeous, decent, sweet nice girl, and for all I know, she could be like this with everyone. Still, I'm drawn to her. I don't know why, but I am.

"Who are the cupcakes for?" I find myself asking. "They smell good."

She blushes. "They're not for anyone exactly. I just felt like baking. Zach always comes over and eats them or my friend April. Grim drops by every now and again, too."

I don't know what she's blushing over exactly, but I smile at her in an attempt to make her more comfortable around me.

"You can eat one from my first batch," she says, watching me expectantly.

I pick up one and take a big bite.

"It's good," I say, moaning softly. "Really good."

I don't know if it tastes so good just because I know she made it, but either way, it just melts in my mouth. Vanilla with choc chips. I approve.

"Thanks," she says, ducking her head. "They're easy enough to make. Anyone could do it."

"I doubt anyone could," I tell her. "Especially this good."

She glances up and smiles. It hits me straight in the chest.

I don't know why, but I want her to like me even though nothing can ever come of it.

What the hell am I doing here? She knows I left with that chick last night. What must she think of me?

I want her to see who I really am.

Why?

I have no idea.

CHAPTER SIX

TRILLIAN

He's standing in my kitchen.

When it hit seven p.m. with no contact from Zach or Xander, I thought for sure they had changed their plans, yet here he is. He looks good wearing dark jeans and a black t-shirt that fits him just right. I stare at his tattoos for a second, mesmerised by the intricate art.

"Do you have any tattoos?" he asks suddenly, having caught me staring.

I look down at my French manicured nails and shake my head. "No, no tattoos."

I do have a belly ring, though, that I got on my eighteenth birthday, which I think is quite pretty. The timer on the oven goes off, so I turn the oven off and pull out the cupcakes.

"Do you need any help?" he asks, walking over to me. "Or will I ruin the masterpieces if I try?"

My lip curls up at that. "They are easy enough. I'm just going to put some icing and sprinkles on these ones as soon as they've cooled down a little."

We wait and I get him a drink.

"Nice place you have here," he says before he takes a sip of his soda.

I look around. "Thanks. I don't like clutter, which is why it's kind of bare."

And white. Everything was white. My dad liked it that way, and so did I.

"I like it," he murmurs and then takes another sip. I watch his throat work as he swallows. "You have good taste."

"Thank you," I reply, smiling shyly.

When ten minutes passes, he washes his hands in the sink then comes to stand next to me, our shoulders almost touching. Xander is tall, so I have to lift my head up to look at his face. I'm about five-six, so he must be well over six foot. I pass him the icing tube and watch as he carefully swirls icing onto one of the cupcakes, his forehead scrunching in concentration. When he's done, I hand him the sprinkles and let him finish off the cupcake. Then we both work together, decorating all twelve of them as we see fit.

"I don't think this was how you expected your evening to go," I say, my eyes on the cupcake he is icing. He is never going to come to my house again, that's for damn sure.

But he just smiles. "I like watching you do this. I can tell you love it. You seem to be in your element."

"I do love it," I admit, glancing up at him. "Plus, it keeps me busy."

"I'm sorry about your dad," he suddenly says, lifting his hand up and brushing his fingers across my cheek.

"Zach told you about that, huh?" I say, repeating his words from last night. I shiver from his simple touch, from his close proximity. He smells so good, like leather mixed with soap.

"He mentioned it," he replies vaguely. "I may have been asking a few questions about you."

I swallow hard. "And why would you be doing that?"

He licks his bottom lip, and my gaze follows the motion. "Curiosity, I guess."

Right. He's curious.

I picture him exiting the taxi this morning, his hair dishevelled, and the mood is broken. I break eye contact and focus on the cupcakes. "They're all done. Give me a minute to clean up and then we can go to dinner."

He nods, a little stiffly. "Take your time."

I show him where the lounge room is so he can watch TV while he waits, then escape to my bedroom. I change into a black maxi dress and sandals and let my hair down. I washed it after work so it's back to being defiant and curly, but it's going to have to do. I put a little powder on my face and grab my handbag, taking a deep breath before I re-enter the lounge room.

"I'm ready when you are," I say.

He turns the TV off and stands up, taking me in from head to toe. "You look beautiful."

My eyes widen. "Oh... umm... thank you."

His hazel eyes smile back at me. "You're welcome. What do you feel like eating?"

"Anything is fine with me," I say. "I'm easy."

I walk in front of him, wincing.

I'm easy?

Did I have to say that?

Although going by his actions last night, he likes easy.

Pushing away that unpleasant thought, we exit through the front door and I lock it behind me. When I see his bike parked in my driveway, I stop in my tracks, smiling widely in excitement.

"Yes!"

He laughs, head turned in my direction. "I thought you'd like another ride."

"You thought right. You rode here from next door? Lazy much?" I tease.

He chuckles. "It was more for you than me."

"You didn't think I'd want to walk like, what, ten steps to Zach's front door?" I ask as my mouth twitches.

Xander crosses his arms over his chest and winks. "I try to be chivalrous and this is what I get, huh?"

I laugh at that, and then rub my hands together. "Let's get on this bad boy."

His entire body shakes with laughter. "Fuck, you're cute."

He helps me onto the bike and I wrap my arms around him.

I think that's my favourite part.

We come to a stop in front of a popular steak house.

"We didn't decide where to go," he says sheepishly, helping me off the bike. "I remember seeing this place when I was riding in, but if you want to go somewhere else, we can."

"This place is fine," I say. "I've eaten here a couple of times and the food is always good."

I take the helmet off and give it back to him.

"I took the longer way here so you could enjoy the ride."

"I noticed. Thanks, I appreciate it," I tell him. "Maybe I should get my own bike?"

"You liked it that much then?" he asks, shaking his head in amusement.

"I think I did," I admit, even though I know I could never ride one myself. Maybe I'll let Zach ride me around from now on after all, even though the thought of riding with anyone apart from Xander isn't as appealing.

"I'm glad it was me that took your motorcycle virginity," he says casually. I'm glad it's dark because my face is suddenly flushed. "You showed me something and I showed you something."

"What did I show you?" I ask.

He leans down closer to me. "You showed me how to decorate cupcakes."

"You're actually admitting that?" I ask, my mouth twitching again. "I don't know many men that would."

Xander takes my comment in stride, flashing me a smile. "I have nothing to prove, babe. I'm all man. And I don't give a fuck what other people think."

Damn if that isn't attractive as hell.

He holds the door open for me as we walk into the restaurant and gestures for me to take a seat before him in one of the booths. I thank him.

"I hope you're hungry," he says as he picks up a menu.

I am.

The waitress comes over and we place our orders.

"What did you want to do after this?" I ask him. "There's a few places we could check out if you want to go to a bar or something. Or if you want to see some sights around town, we could do that, too."

He glances up at me through his lashes. "Maybe we could watch a movie or something? I don't really want to go out to a bar or club."

I suppose it would be boring to go out to a club with just the two of us. He'd want to find someone to hook up with and I would be left alone. It doesn't seem like a good time.

"Sounds good to me," I say. "I don't really mind, either—"

"Trillian, hey," comes a voice, interrupting my sentence. I look to the right and see Richard standing there as he stares at Xander. "I thought you said you were single."

My eyes narrow slightly. "I am single, not that I should be explaining myself."

He doesn't take his eyes from Xander. "I'm Richard, a friend of Trillian's."

"Xander."

I lean back against the red leather bench and wish Richard would just leave. "I just thought I'd say hi since our conversation was interrupted today."

I can feel Xander's gaze on me, so I turn my head to look at him.

He looks amused, like he's enjoying the show.

"Richard, could we talk about this another time, please?" I ask, hoping he will drop it for now.

"Of course," he says. "I'll probably see you around anyway. Enjoy your night."

He walks away and I feel bad.

"I'm a horrible person," I mutter, covering my face with my hands.

Xander chuckles. "No, you're not. You weren't rude to him even though he deserved it."

Our drinks arrive and I'm grateful for the distraction.

"Is he an ex of yours or something?" he asks after a sip of his soft drink.

I shake my head. "No, I don't even know him, really. He comes into my work all the time and seems nice enough, but I'm not interested in him like that. I don't want to hurt his feelings or lead him on, so I'm obviously going to have to have a talk with him."

Xander reaches out his hand and places it on mine, his thumb rubbing gently. Leaning forward over the table, he says, "Maybe he will see this and get the picture."

"See what?" I ask quietly, staring down at his hand.

"This," he murmurs, before his lips come down on mine, catching me unaware. It's just a quick kiss with no tongue, just a press of his lips on mine, but I'm still left feeling breathless.

And speechless.

CHAPTER SEVEN

TRILLIAN

"Trill?"

"Hmmm?" I reply, studying my orange juice.

"Are you going to give me the silent treatment now?" he asks.

I glance up and sigh. "You just kissed me."

"I know," he says, amusement playing on his features. "I was there. And I have to say I've been thinking of doing it ever since I laid eyes on you."

I don't know what to say to that.

If that's true, why the hell did he spend the night with someone else?

Like I need that reminder.

The waitress brings our food to the table. Xander ordered a huge steak, ribs, mashed potatoes, and salad while I went with the creamy chicken dish. I keep my eyes on my food, but I can feel his on me.

"How is it?" he finally asks.

I swallow my bite then raise my eyes to his. "Really good. How's yours?"

He licks his bottom lip. "It's amazing. Do you want a bite? You have to try this."

"No, thanks," I reply, forking a piece of chicken.

"Aww, come on," he says, grinning playfully. He cuts a small piece of steak and smothers some mashed potato on top, and then lifts his fork to me, a challenging look in his eyes. I open my mouth as he slowly feeds me, flavours bursting on my tongue as I close my mouth and chew.

"It's good," I tell him after I swallow. "Really good."

He gazes at my mouth. "It's delicious, isn't it? Like nothing I've tasted before. And trust me, I've had my fair share."

I don't think we're still talking about the steak.

Nervously, I lick my lips, and I don't miss the hitch in his breath. The tension between us suddenly reaches new heights.

What does he want from me?

Whatever it is, he could get it from any woman.

I look back down at my plate and Xander clears his throat.

"Any movies in mind?" I ask.

He leans back against the booth and flashes a boyish, lopsided smile. "Lady's choice."

"You might live to regret that," I tease. "Are you sure you trust my judgement?"

"Positive," he says confidently. "I have a feeling that you, Trillian, are full of surprises."

"I think you're making me out to be a lot more interesting than I actually am," I tell him, giving him a pointed look before taking a sip of my drink.

His full lips quirk at the corners. Why do I always amuse him?

"Do you want to order dessert?" he asks, glancing at my almost empty plate. "Or can we go back to your house and eat the rest of those cupcakes?"

That makes me smile.

"You really want to do that?" I ask. "We could always watch movies at my house."

Xander sits up straighter. "You wouldn't mind?"

"Why would I?" I ask, tilting my head to the side.

He shrugs. "I don't know. Never mind. I'm not going to question it. I'm ready to leave when you are."

"Xander?"

"Yes, Trillian?"

I love the way he says my name.

"Can we take an even longer way home?" I ask, unable to mask the hope in my voice.

His eyes soften. "Yeah, of course, we can."

He pays for dinner.

I argue.

I lose.

Then we go back to my house for cupcakes and movies.

Tonight is turning out like nothing I expected.

"Are you close with your mum?" I ask him, bringing my knees up to my chest. We're both sitting on either side of my grey couch, facing each other, movie long forgotten while playing in the background. After an hour-long ride on the back of his bike, we came home and had dessert, then retreated to the lounge room for movies and hot chocolate. Xander is a good listener, and for some reason, I'm starting to feel comfortable around him, which isn't always an easy feat.

"I guess," he replies. "I've always been closer with my dad, though."

"How long are you staying in Channon?"

He puts his mug down on the coffee table and gazes into my eyes. "Depends."

"Depends on what?"

His eyes crinkle, but he doesn't answer the question, instead asking one of his own. "Do you get lonely living here by yourself?"

I shake my head. "I'm used to it. Plus, Zach and Grim are next door if I need anything."

"You should get a dog," he says. "A guard dog."

I smirk. "I live next door to the president of the Channon chapter the Wind Dragons MC and his reckless son. Who would be stupid enough to rob this house?"

He laughs at that. "Fuck, you're right. But still, it never hurts to be careful."

"Are you worried about me, Xander?" I ask, grinning. "I was going to full name you, but I don't even know your surname."

"It's Kane," he says.

"Xander Kane," I say, testing the words. "I like it."

He moves his leg so it's now touching mine. My eyes dart from our legs back up to his face.

"Any plans tomorrow?"

"Just studying, I guess."

"What are you studying?" he asks, seeming genuinely interested.

"Bachelor of Education." I bite the inside of my cheek as he leans forward, getting close enough to me that I can smell his cologne.

He nods slightly. "I think you would make an amazing teacher."

"And why is that?"

"You're patient and kind," he says. "I could already tell that about you, even if Zach didn't go on about how fuckin' amazing you are every chance he gets."

I can't help but laugh at that. "Is that what he says about me when I'm not around? Good to know. What do you do with yourself back in Perth?"

"My dad owned his own motorcycle shop, which is now mine. So I run that business, plus I'm also a mechanic."

"Who's looking after the business then?"

"My friend Dash is keeping an eye on things for me," Xander replies. "I have good people that work there, I trust them. They've been working for my dad for a long time. My sister, Summer, pops in from time to time as well."

"Sounds nice."

"It is. Hasn't been the same since Dad left though, which is why I wanted to get away. And I'm glad I did."

I hear the sadness in his voice and it makes my own heart hurt. For him and for myself because I still miss my own dad every day. I also don't miss that he said his dad left, instead of passed.

Was he in denial?

"Is it true what they say?" he suddenly asks.

"Is what true?"

"Does time heal?"

I know what he's asking. He wants to know if, as time passes, will the pain of losing someone he loved disappear.

"I guess, in a way, you learn to deal with the pain. It does lessen as you accept things. So time does heal all wounds, just not completely. Nothing can do that. You learn to live with the scars and soon forget they're there, but they never disappear completely."

He nods like I've confirmed something he already knows. "Dad loved Channon. It feels nice being here. A change, you know?"

"It's a peaceful place," I say. "For the most part, you know, besides being the home of a badass motorcycle club."

Xander grins. "You're fuckin' cute, do you know that?"

His hair is tied back in a bun today and I can't help but find it extremely sexy. My gaze wanders down his arms, his tattoos, and huge, strong hands.

"Do you like what you see?" he asks quietly, not in a cocky tone, but a serious one. Does he really want to know if I find him attractive? I don't think there's a woman alive that wouldn't.

"I do," I admit, my cheeks feeling flushed. I look down, a little shy. "You know I do."

He slides over, closing the space between us and lifts my face up to meet his with his finger under my chin. "How do I know that you do?"

I decide to be honest with him and talk about the big elephant in the room. "When I saw you at the bar, I thought you were the most handsome man I'd ever seen in my life, but you didn't want me, did you? You left with someone else, but that's okay. I mean, we can be friends. I like hanging around you."

He curses, then lowers his lips to mine and kisses me, sucking on my lower lip, and then drawing it into his mouth. His tongue slides into my mouth, tentatively at first, then more demanding. His hands cup my face while mine rest on his rock hard chest, clutching his shirt. I don't think about anything except what I'm feeling, the taste and smell of him.

He is such a good kisser.

He pulls away before I'm ready and I moan in protest.

He gazes into my eyes. "Listen to me, Trill. I've never seen a woman as beautiful as you. Never. And you're so fuckin' sweet you could make a man lose himself. Leaving with someone else was fuckin' stupid, but I did it because I thought I couldn't have you."

I blink a few times, still feeling dazed by his kisses.

"I fucked up, Trill," he says when I stay silent, still trying to make sense of everything.

"What am I doing?" I ask as my heart races.

What the fuck am I doing? Can I just have a one-night stand with him? I've never had one before, and I'm not sure I can without getting hurt in the end. I don't feel good about even considering this when he was with another woman just last night. Apparently, when it comes to Xander, I have no shame or dignity.

"Trillian—"

"Last night, your mouth was on someone else, and now I'm letting you kiss me and enjoying it. What the hell does that say about me?"

Without warning, Xander lifts me up and puts me on his lap. I can feel his hardness pressing against me, but he doesn't say anything and neither do I. I'm too upset and confused to feel anything else.

"Now are you going to listen to me?" he asks, his tone laced with steel.

I nod.

I'm going to listen, but I also know I'm not going to like what he has to say.

CHAPTER EIGHT

XANDER

How does a man say sorry to a woman he wants because he was between another woman's thighs just the night before? There isn't any way around this. I fucked up big time and nothing I say will fix it.

What changed between last night and tonight? Last night, Trillian was just a beautiful woman I was drawn to and someone I thought was off limits. Tonight, Trillian is someone I can see myself with for a lot more than a simple fuck. I like being around her and I want to get to know her better. I want to know everything about her. Trillian is angry with herself because she allowed herself to kiss me when I, like a stupid shit, was with someone else last night. If only I had just kept it in my pants. Fuck. I don't know how to solve this, but there is one thing I can do to buy me some time and keep her around me.

So I do it.

"I'm going to be straight with you. I wanted you, I thought I couldn't have you, so I played it off and left with someone else. Yes, I fucked her, but it didn't mean anything, it was just sex. I felt like shit afterward, even though I shouldn't have because we'd only met once and that was it. But it was you I wanted, not her or anyone else."

I take a breath, watching the expressions play on her face and wondering what the hell she is thinking.

"I like you, Trillian, and I want to get to know you better," I say, now in a quieter tone. "I know I'm only here for a little while, but I want to spend that time with you."

She opens those pouty lips of hers. "You want a casual fling with me then, until you have to leave?"

Is that what I want? It's all that makes sense really, given the situation. It isn't like I can offer her anything else. She didn't sound offended when she said *casual fling*. It just sounds like she wanted to understand exactly what it is I want from her.

"We don't have to label it, Trill," I say. "Do you like being around me? Do you want to be around me? That's all it really comes down to. After spending tonight with you, I don't think I could sit at Zach's without wanting to be here."

She scrapes her teeth along her bottom lip. "I do want to be around you."

I exhale with relief. I don't know what I would do if she didn't or how I would accept it.

You just met her, calm the fuck down.

"I don't expect anything from you, Trill," I say, in case she thinks I'm going to take her to her room and have my way with her as soon as an agreement passes her lips. Not that I don't want to be with her in that way because, fuck, I do—my throbbing dick is a testament to that, but I'm not going to—at least, not tonight when I know she is thinking about Paula… or whatever the fuck her name was.

"I want you to trust me."

When she sighs and lays her head against my chest, I know that I've won. I kiss the top of her head, smiling. I won't rush her. I'll just enjoy my time with her before I have to go home. Running a hand down her back, I relax back into the couch.

"Can I make you breakfast in the morning?" I ask, wanting to do something nice for her.

She lifts her head. "You cook?"

I kiss her cheek. "I do okay in the kitchen."

"Expect Zach to join us," she mumbles. "There's no way he won't be here on a Sunday morning expecting to be fed."

I chuckle. "Noted."

I need to talk to him about Trillian. I don't know how he'll react, but I'm hoping he'll be okay with it. I got the feeling from him that he liked the idea, but I don't know why. Zach knows me well. He used to live in Perth until he moved to Channon. After that, he and Grim did annual trips down to visit Dad and me when they were on club business. We've gotten up to a lot of shit over the years, things I'm sure he wouldn't have told anyone about, especially Trillian.

I glance down at her to find her eyes closed. It's about one am, so she must be exhausted after going out last night and then working all day today. I don't like the thought of leaving her here alone to go next door, but I don't think she'd like the idea of me sleeping over tonight. I really wanted to, though. It feels right somehow.

I stand with her in my arms and walk toward her bedroom. Opening the door, I step to the bed and pull the red quilt down, then place her on the bed and tuck her in. The first time being in her room, I glance around before leaning down and kissing her mouth softly.

I pull back when she stirs.

"Xander?"

"Yeah, Trill," I whisper. "Go to sleep. I'll lock the door on the way out."

She opens her bright blue eyes and frowns sleepily. "Can't you sleep here tonight?"

I swallow hard, wanting nothing more than to slide in next to her. "Are you sure?"

She nods her head. "Just to sleep, I mean."

I hide my smile. "Just to sleep. I want to, Trill, but I don't know…"

"We're just sleeping next to each other, Xander," she says.

Deciding she's right, I pull my t-shirt off and watch her eyes widen as she takes me in. I stifle the urge to flex. Instead, I take off my jeans, leaving me in my boxer shorts. Smirking at the look on her face, I can't help but tease her.

"Change your mind?"

She shakes her head, her gaze glued to my abs.

"I can't sleep in my jeans. It would be uncomfortable," I explain, growing hard under her perusal. Fuck, the way she looks at me, like she's never seen a man before, like she'd like nothing more than to lick me from head to toe, makes me need to have a cold fuckin' shower.

She scoots over in the bed, pulls the blanket down, and closes her eyes again. I slide in next to her, and she instantly melts against my body. When she slides her thigh in between mine, I look at the ceiling and try not to groan.

Fuck.

I could get used to this.

After a good night's sleep, I get up before Trillian and head back over to Zach's to shower, brush my teeth, and change clothes. Zach walks in the door as I'm about to go back to her house.

"Hey," he grins, his eyes bloodshot.

"What happened to you?" I ask with raised eyebrows.

He collapses on the couch and lifts his legs up onto the coffee table. "Wild party. When I say wild, I mean wild. Fuck, Sin and his men know how to party. That Rake is a fuckin' machine. A pussy machine."

I laugh at that. "Sounds like an interesting man."

"You have no idea. Men like them, Sin and Arrow, fuck, wouldn't want to mess with them. Glad they're on our side."

I didn't want to get into his biker politics, but I find myself asking, "Why, are they higher up than you?"

Zach shakes his head. "They're just from a different chapter. Where you live, actually. I'll have to introduce you one day. I forget you don't know everyone."

"Sounds good. You know you look like you've been to hell and back," I tell him, amused by his appearance.

"How was your night?" he asks, studying me. "How's my girl?"

His girl?

I think not.

Not anymore, at least.

"Went out for dinner, a bike ride, and watched some movies," I say, sitting next to him.

He sits up straighter. "Trillian let you take her on your bike?"

I nod, not telling him about how she got on the night of the club. "Yeah, and she fuckin' loves it."

"Fuck off," he breathes. "She wasn't scared? I've been trying to get her on my bike for years. And just like that, she lets you? She and I are going to have words."

My eyes narrow on him. "You fuckin' won't be having words with her about it."

His eyes widen, and then he smiles. A slow-spreading smile that makes me nervous. "You like her."

I glance away and sigh. "I do. Fuck, she's everything I've ever wanted in a woman and never found. But it's more than that—I can't even explain it. I just want to protect her."

And fuck her like crazy, but that's another story.

Zach laughs. "Fuck, only Trillian could tame someone like you."

"Me? Tamed? Not fuckin' likely," I deny. We've only just met. It isn't possible. "And 'someone like me?'" I ask, even though I know what he means.

I love women.

And I've loved them ever since I turned fifteen.

A lot.

But this thing with Trillian is different. I don't just want sex from her. I want her. I want everything—things that have never crossed my mind before.

"You know what I mean, Xander. I'm not saying I'm any better. I just don't want to see Trill hurt. You're one of my best friends, but Trill is, too, and Trill needs me, so you better know that I'll be there for her no matter what."

I'm not mad that he's essentially saying he'll choose Trill over me if I fuck up. I'm glad, because Trillian deserves someone to be there for her. "I got you."

"Good," he replies. "She needs a good man. She deserves one."

"I know. We're going to be seeing each other while I'm here," I say, rubbing the back of my neck. "I don't know what's going to happen, but I like being with her."

"She's sweet as fuck, isn't she," Zach murmurs. "Kindest heart I've ever known."

I stand. "I told her I'd make her breakfast."

Zach stares at me a second then starts laughing. When he starts making whipping sounds, I decide to get out of there. I head to the store to grab a few things, unsure what Trillian has. Now back at her house, I knock on the door, my hands full of groceries.

CHAPTER NINE

TRILLIAN

After spending the night in his arms, I wake up alone. I don't know how I feel about that. However, about an hour later, Xander is back at my front door, his arms full of groceries. Wide-eyed, I let him in and sit on the kitchen counter top as he makes an omelette with a side of bacon.

I've never had a man besides my dad cook for me before. It's definitely something I could get used to.

*****

"Zach messaged and wants to go for a ride tonight. Do you want to come?" Xander asks as he unscrews the lid on his water bottle. It's a warm day today, so we decided to go to the beach. We're both sitting on our towels on the sand after just having come out of the water. Xander is bare-chested, rivulets of water dripping down his smooth, tanned chest. My mouth is dry.

"Trill?"

Oh, right, he asked me a question. His body is making me stupid. "Are you sure you don't want to spend some alone time with Zach?"

"I'll be with Zach all day tomorrow while you're at uni," he replies, tilting his head back and drinking. I watch his throat work as he swallows, and I suddenly feel the need to fan myself. I glance around and see that I'm not the only woman to notice the fine specimen sitting next to me. In fact, any female within the ages of fifteen to sixty on the beach seems to be watching him. I glance at Xander, who is now looking at me, either oblivious to all the attention or used to it.

"Maybe you should put a shirt on," I mock-whisper. "You're creating a spectacle."

"What?" he asks, mouth twitching. "You should talk. Any male that walks this way zooms in on your tits and ass."

My mouth drops open. "That's not true."

I'm wearing a one-piece swimsuit, but the sides are cut out, showing a little of my stomach. It doesn't show much cleavage, but obviously, every flaw on my body can be seen. I walked out with a t-shirt over it, until we were about to get into the water and Xander asked me to raise my arms and he pulled it off. He assumed I wasn't going to swim in a t-shirt and I didn't correct him. He'd smiled at me then lowered his gaze, taking me in, before reaching his hand out and leading me to the water. He didn't make a big deal out of anything or make me feel too awkward about him seeing me in something so revealing for the first time.

"It is true," he murmurs, "but I can't say that I blame them."

"Smooth talker," I mumble, causing him to chuckle.

"Just the truth, babe," he replies, leaning back on his elbows.

"There you are," comes a voice from behind me. April plops down next to me, sitting on the sand. She looks to Xander. "Hello, sexy stranger from the other night."

He nods, his eyes crinkling. "April."

I look at my best friend. "I thought you were going to be here an hour ago."

"And I thought you would have called me with juicy gossip about why you're hanging out with him," she says, wiggling her finely arched blonde eyebrows. "Are you finally getting some action?"

I sigh heavily. I'm used to her lack of filter, but did she have to say that in front of Xander? Her eyes sparkle. Of course, she did. "Why are we friends again?"

I glance at Xander to see him watching our banter with amusement.

"Because you love me," April replies in a singsong voice and then adjusts her ice blue bikini top. "Where are all the hot guys today? I swear, they're all in hiding."

"They probably heard you were on the prowl," I fire back, smirking.

She rolls her eyes. "If they heard I was on the prowl, they'd be lining up."

Looking to Xander, she says, "So I heard you're a friend of Zach's. How long are you in town?"

Xander glances at me before replying. "Not sure yet, maybe a week or so."

Before, he'd said a few days, so a week was an improvement.

Staring into the water, I squint when I see a familiar mop of reddish-brown hair. "Is that Zach in the water?"

Xander and April both look along my line of sight.

Yes, it's Zach. He's chest deep in the ocean, his mouth all over some woman.

"When did he even get here?" I ask, wondering why we're only just seeing him.

April sniffs. "Who knows with him? He's an easy pussy magnet. If it's easy, he's there."

Something once happened between Zach and April, but neither of them will speak of it. Things were awkward for a while, but now they're back to being friends. However, whenever April has to actually see him with another woman, this side of her comes out. I personally think they hooked up and Zach ran scared. It sounds like him. I don't think he wants to be in a long-term relationship right now, or at least that's what he's said in the past. I'm curious, but I don't want to pry. April will tell me if she wants me to know.

Xander chuckles. "He's single and likes to enjoy life."

April glares at him. "Of course, you'll stand up for him."

I stand up and dust the sand off my ass. "Is it safe to go back into the water?"

"What do you mean?" Xander asks, also standing up.

I point to Zach, who I'm pretty sure is having sex in the ocean.

In the open.

In broad daylight.

"Fucking hell, there could be kids around here," April growls, standing up and crossing her arms over her chest. "Do you guys want to get something to eat?"

My stomach chooses that moment to growl, as if it heard what April was saying and was answering for me.

"We'll take that as a yes," Xander says, casually wrapping his arm around my shoulder. "Come on, let's get you fed."

April glances over at me and mouths the word 'hot'. I shake my head at her and mouth 'stop it' back to her. She grins and quickly catches up to us, coming on the other side of me and threading her arm through mine.

"So, Xander," she starts, her tone casual, but I know her better. "What is it that you do for a living exactly?"

And let the best friend interrogation begin.

*****

"Do you have any children?" she asks him, making me almost choke on my French fry.

"No," Xander replies patiently. "No kids."

"That you know of," April says in a quieter voice.

My eyes narrow on her. "April, seriously?"

She shrugs and leans back against her chair. "Just making conversation. I have a shift at the bar tonight so I better get going. Are we still having lunch tomorrow after your class?"

I nod. "We are. I'll meet you there around one."

"Sounds good," she says, standing. "Nice seeing you again, Xander."

"You too, April," Xander says in a friendly tone.

She leans down and kisses me on my cheek. "See you."

"Drive safely."

"I will," she says, exiting the café.

"She cares about you a lot," Xander says, watching me with a warm look on his face. "Everyone who knows you does."

"I know," I reply. "I'm lucky that way. Don't have that many friends, but the ones I do have are amazing."

"You don't have any other family around here?" he asks, pushing his fork around his plate.

"My dad's sister and my cousins live in Melbourne, and some of my mother's family lives in Sydney, but I don't talk to them," I say. I don't talk to anyone on my mum's side, but I do talk to my aunty and cousins every month or so.

"They didn't want you to come and live with them?" he asks. "I'm not judging, just trying to understand."

"Understand what?" I ask, leaning my chin on the inside of my hand.

"How they are okay with you being here by yourself. I know you have Zach, Grim, and April, but still, you were how old when your dad passed away?"

"Twenty."

"Right, twenty. Still a baby."

"My aunty did want me to go there, but I said no. I wasn't leaving my house. It's the last thing of my dad's that I have. I grew up here and have so many memories in that house," I explain.

He nods like he understands and I guess maybe he does.

"You didn't ask about my mum, so I'm assuming Zach said something to you," I say, wringing my hands.

He takes one of my hands in his and rubs his thumb on my knuckles. "He mentioned that she left and you haven't seen her since."

I swallow hard and look down. "Haven't seen or heard from her. I think being a wife and mother wasn't the life she thought it was going to be. My dad was a trucker, so he would work away sometimes, and she was left in the house alone with me. My dad wasn't rich and I don't think she liked that either."

"It was her loss," he says softly. "Look what you became without her. You're smart, responsible, sweet. And beautiful."

My eyes lift to his. "You really think that, don't you?"

He grins. "I wouldn't be sitting here right now if I didn't."

"Oh, really," I croon. "And where exactly would you be? In the ocean with Zach and another woman?"

A strange look passes over his face. "What was that look?"

"What look?"

"I don't know… you had an odd look on your face."

He leans forward and kisses my knuckles. "Just thinking. Do you want to get out of here?"

I nod. "Yeah, I'm full. Oh, and I'm paying this time."

He laughs, rubbing his chest. "It's cute that you think so."

I open my mouth and then close it. "I don't think so. I know so. It's about time you let me have my way, Xander Kane."

"I'll always let you have your way, but not in this," he says, standing up and reaching his hand out to me. "I have to say, you're the first woman to complain so much about me paying for everything."

I grit my teeth. "A little advice? It's not smart to bring up other women around the girl you're…" I trail off. What the hell am I saying? We aren't dating. Shit, this is awkward. I hope he doesn't call me out on it, but he does.

"The girl I'm what?" he asks, pulling me out of my chair and against his warm chest. He had put on a white cotton t-shirt with his board shorts.

"Friends with," I add, sounding like an idiot.

He cups my face and lifts it up so I have no choice, but to look into his eyes. "Friends? I want to be much more than friends with you, Trillian."

"You do?" I ask, blinking.

"You know I do," he replies. "I'm just waiting until the right time."

"We don't exactly have all the time in the world, you know," I point out.

He lowers his head and kisses my mouth gently, a barely there caress. "I know. But I fucked it up when I did what I did, and now I'm not going to be with you until I know you know you're different. You're nothing like any of the other women I've been with."

"There you go again, mentioning other women," I mumble, pouting a little.

He kisses my mouth again then pulls back. "I haven't been a saint, Trill, you need to know that. I'm young, and yeah, I've had my share of women, but like I said, you're different."

"Why?" I ask.

His gaze lowers to my mouth. "Fuck if I know. I just want you more than I've ever wanted someone before. That's all I know."

I squeeze my thighs together. Fuck, his speech is turning me on. Just what I need, considering he's just talking about how he isn't going to take me to bed until he decides the timing is right. I decide to be a little bold, pushing him as far as he'll go. Standing on my tiptoes, I kiss his jaw, and then whisper into his ear, "What if I want you? We could go home right now, get into my bed, and stay there until tomorrow morning."

His eyes flash, and his hands tighten on my waist.

"We're going home," he says. "Now."

He takes my hand and leads me out to his bike.

I follow, anticipation spreading through my veins.

I want him… and I'm going to get him.

CHAPTER TEN

XANDER

You can't fuck her.

You can't fuck her.

I repeat this over and over in my head as we ride home, but her sweet body pressed against my back isn't helping. I want her, badly, but I know that if we sleep together, she'll think she's just like the girl from the other night.

She isn't.

And it's important for her to know that.

I'm trying to be a gentleman, but she's pushing me. I want nothing more than to lay her back on her bed and devour her with my mouth before fucking her like she's never been fucked before. I want to make her come over and over, scream my name, and hear her beg for more. I want to own her, possess her, and it scares me a little. I've never felt like this for any other woman, even Persephone, who at one point I thought maybe could have been something long term.

Trillian runs her hands over my stomach, feeling my muscles and making my semi hard-on turn into a full-fledged one. She has a power over me that I normally wouldn't like, because you can't trust all women. Just like you can't trust all men, I suppose. But with her, I know, I just know she's good down to her bones. I can see it in her, in the way people around her treat her and in how she treats them. If I have to be owned by any woman, Trillian is a good choice. The best choice. In fact, I feel like I won the fuckin' lottery.

She leans even closer against my back, and for once, I wish I were off the bike so I could wrap my arms around her and bury my face in her neck. Kiss her from head to toe. I can't lie to myself—I want a taste of her. Of her mouth, her pussy. I want to suck on those breasts of hers, squeeze the globes of her bare ass.

In my head, I torture myself by planning out exactly what I want to do to her. The bike comes to a stop in her driveway, and I'm about to pull her off the bike and drag her inside like a caveman when I realise we're not alone. I do a double take when I see who is standing, his arms crossed, watching me from Zach's driveway.

Dread hits my stomach.

Something must be wrong. Why else would Ryan Knox be standing before me—in Channon?

"Do you know that guy?" Trillian asks, her brows drawn together.

"Yeah, I do," I say. "Can you do me a favour and go inside? I'll be there in a second."

"Is everything okay?" she asks, sounding worried.

I lick my lips. "I don't know. That's Summer's brother-in-law, and if he's here, it must be something important."

"Okay," she says. "I hope everything is okay."

I kiss her forehead before she walks to her front door, and I wait until she's safely inside before I walk over to where Ryan is leaning against his car.

"What's happened?" I ask as I stand before him. "Is Summer okay?"

"Hello to you, too," he says without the usual sparkle in his eye. "We tried calling you, but you haven't been answering your phone."

Oh, right.

Fuck.

I put it on silent last night, then forgot it at Zach's this morning when I went to get changed.

"Talk to me."

"You need to come home, Xander," he says without blinking. "Now."

Fuck.

*****

I pack up all my shit at Zach's house, give him a call explaining the situation, then head over to Trillian's house. I have to leave. Summer is in the hospital, and it isn't good. I'm not sure how she's going to handle something like this, but I know she needs me to be there for her. I scowl when I find Trill's front door unlocked. walk inside and find her in the kitchen where she turns to me with a wide-eyed look.

"What happened?" she asks quietly.

"I need to go back home," I tell her. "My sister Summer is in the hospital."

She gasps. "Is she okay? I'm so sorry, Xander."

I step to her and wrap her in my arms, burying my face in her neck.

Peace.

I feel peaceful when I'm around this woman.

"I need to leave, Trillian," I whisper. "Right now."

She rubs my back. "Of course you do, Xander."

I lift my head up, staring down at her. "Do you want to come?"

I don't want to let her out of my sight. She could come back with me and spend some time with me. We could get to know each other better. I can't explain it, I just don't want to say goodbye to her.

"I… I have uni and work," she stutters. "I can't just leave. Though I wish I could."

I sigh. Of course. Her life is here. I can't expect her to drop everything to come back with me, no matter how much I want her to. I lower my lips to hers and give her a goodbye kiss. She opens her mouth eagerly, her arms reaching around my neck, pulling me down to her. She tastes sweet, and I wish I had the time to show her just how much I want her, but I don't. I pull away and kiss along her jawline, then place one kiss on her collarbone.

"I have to go," I tell her. "I'll call you, okay? I'll be back whenever I can."

She smiles sadly, looking like she doesn't believe me. "Go, Xander, your family needs you right now."

Another quick, almost desperate kiss, and then I walk out the door.

*****

Summer was pregnant. She hadn't told anyone except her husband, Reid. She was waiting for the three-month mark but has lost the baby at two months. She isn't taking it very well, as would be expected. After riding back to Perth, I went home for a quick shower then straight to the hospital. Ryan didn't tell me the exact details; just that Summer had lost a baby and was asking for me. When I walk into the hospital room, my sister sits there staring straight ahead. At nothing. Her face is blank, her normally bright eyes dull.

"Summer?"

She turns her head to me. "Xander, you came."

Her voice comes out cracked, broken, like she hasn't used it much.

I walk to her bed, pull a chair from the side, and sit next to her, taking her hand in mine. "Of course I came. You know I'm always here for you."

She looks down at our hands. "I lost her."

"I know," I reply on a whisper. "I know."

I don't know what to say. It will be okay? You can always try again, have more children? The comments seem insensitive. Instead, I stand, moving next to her on the bed, and pull her into my arms. She starts to cry, her body shaking with each heart-wrenching sob. I lift my head to see Reid standing in the doorway, his eyes red, and his body stiff. I know that each tear Summer sheds kills him. The man is so in love with her. It's like nothing I've ever seen before, and I can tell how much this is hurting him. His posture and expression scream defeat. He nods at me, and then leaves the room. I kiss Summer on top of her head.

"We'll get through this, okay? We always do." My voice is barely a whisper.

She wipes her wet eyes with my t-shirt. "Thanks for coming back. I know you were on holiday trying to work out your own shit."

"Don't you worry about all that, Sum," I reply. "How was Channon?"

Trillian's face flashes before my eyes. "Fuckin' beautiful."

She lifts her face and studies me. "What happened over there?"

I rub the back of my neck. "I think we have other things to discuss, don't you?"

She rolls her eyes. "Are you kidding me? What I need right now is a distraction. I don't want to think about what I've lost and what a failure I am."

My body stills at that. "You aren't a failure, Summer, and don't say that again."

She sighs. "Fine. Tell me about Channon. I know Dad loved that place."

"He did love it. I stayed with Zach, which was nice. There was a girl I met…"

I trail off as I see a spark of the Summer I know. She rubs her hands together and narrows her eyes. "This ought to be interesting."

"Are you going to let me talk or keep interrupting me?"

She smirks. "Keep interrupting you. So who was she? Did you bone?"

My mouth twitches. "Trillian. Her name is Trillian."

CHAPTER ELEVEN

TRILLIAN

ONE MONTH LATER

I cut a slice of red velvet cake and put it on my plate. At this rate, my ass is going to be the size of a house. I usually don't eat much of what I bake, besides the odd taste here and there or the casual cupcake, but suddenly, I'm making up for it. I'm eating everything. To be fair, though, I now run in the morning and the evening, so I keep up with my fitness routine.

"The guys at the clubhouse are going to want to marry you after tasting these cakes," Zach says, talking with a giant piece of said cake in his mouth.

I grin. "Are you ever going to take me into the clubhouse?"

I didn't know why I wanted to go, but I was curious. And I could use a distraction.

He chews thoughtfully and then swallows before answering. "If you really want to go, I'll take you. But the men will want you and some of the things you see will shock you. Are you ready for that? 'Cause if you look at me differently, I'm gonna be pissed."

I roll my eyes. "Do you think I'm stupid? I know what happens there. Do you think I don't hear the women talk?"

He licks cake off his bottom lip. "Fine. You can come with me now to drop off the cakes."

It's one of the members' old lady's birthday and I'd made three different cakes for everyone at the club.

"Are you going to wear that?" Zach asks, taking in my jean shorts and tank top.

"Are people going to be dressed up?" I ask, frowning. Maybe I'll put on a dress or something.

Zach chuckles deeply. "It's casual, it's just that your ass looks good in those and I really don't want to have to fight off men today."

I purse my lips. "Why are your eyes on my ass, Zach?"

His eyes twinkle. "Oh, please, it's not like anyone can miss it. Everywhere I look, it's like, bam! In my face."

I rub my forehead. "Is that so? Whatever. You know, I heard you got your dick pierced."

He chokes on his cake, and I actually have to hit him on his back, maybe a little harder than necessary.

"Who the fuck told you that?" he asks when he can finally speak.

"Like I said," I say, "women talk. And women also like ice cream. I hear a lot of shit, most recently about you having an interesting piercing down there. Oh, and apparently you shared this woman with one of your club brothers."

Zach cringes and glances at me. "Fine, I won't make any more comments about your ass."

"I'd appreciate that," I reply dryly. "Let me get changed and then we can go."

He groans. "You don't have to change. It's fine. Are you going to ride on the back of my bike?"

I hadn't been on a bike since Xander left. He'd called me twice in a month.

Only twice.

I messaged him a few times, and he messaged back, but he never said anything about whether he was coming back. I take that as a bad sign. He is obviously busy with his sister, whom I hope is doing okay, but I don't know where we stand and it's driving me crazy. I'm overthinking everything.

Analysing our time together.

It's stupid.

"We can't take your bike. We're carrying three cakes," I point out.

Zack chuckles. "Oh, yeah. Good point. We'll go in my car then."

"Okay, sounds good to me," I say, grabbing my handbag from where I threw it on the couch. "Ready when you are."

I lock up the house and walk over to Zach's car. "Have you spoken to Xander?"

He unlocks the doors with a click of a button and I slide in, holding the chocolate mud cake on my lap. Zach puts the two cakes he's carrying in the back seat.

"A few days ago," I reply when he sits in the driver's seat.

"I'm sure he'll be back. Dude was practically in love with you," he says, shaking his head in astonishment. "Never seen him so into a woman."

"I seriously doubt that," I reply, sighing and looking out the window as the car starts and reverses. "It wasn't going to work out, anyway. I'm not going to leave Channon and his family and business are in Perth. Maybe it's for the best that he left as soon as he did."

"Do you really think that?" Zach asks quietly.

I shrug. "I don't know what to think."

"Hmmm."

"Hmmm, what?" I ask him.

"Well, then, maybe if you and Xander are over, you might be interested in one of the Wind Dragons members."

My head snaps to him. "Yeah, I don't think so."

"And why not?" he asks, sounding smug. "We aren't all that bad and you'd make a hell of an old lady."

I sigh. "I can't even think of another man right now. In that short time, Xander has done a number on me. No one is him. No one will ever be him. How the hell did he make me feel so comfortable around him so soon?"

"I fuckin' knew it!" Zach replies. "If you want him, why don't you do a trip to Perth and tell him? I'll take you if you want."

I look to him. "You'd do that? What if he doesn't want me there?"

"Then he's an asshole who doesn't deserve you. But trust me, he'd want you there. He's been calling me to make sure I'm keeping an eye on you. Like I haven't been doing that for the last few fuckin' years."

He can call Zach but can't find the time to call me? Now I was even angrier.

"I can take care of myself."

"I know, Trill, I know."

"I'll think about it," I say. "So tonight is Gina's birthday, right? And she's Poison's old lady?"

Zach nods. "Yep. Gina's turning thirty-five. She's gonna love the cakes."

"How many people are going to be there?" I ask, staring down at the cake in my hands.

"Ummm, I don't know, maybe fifty people."

We spend the rest of the drive in comfortable silence.

When Zach turns right into the compound, I take in the building, my eyes scanning it greedily. I've driven past it, of course, but never been inside the gates.

Zach laughs. "Look at you."

I turn to him with a sheepish smile playing on my lips. "I've been curious for a while now."

"I can see that," he murmurs. "Dad's not gonna be happy about me bringing you here."

I sit up straighter at that. "Why not?"

"You're like the daughter he always wanted but never had."

"So? These are his men, right. I mean, he is the president," I say, not understanding.

Zach chuckles. "Yes, that's true, but come on. Sending you in here is like dangling a mouse in front of a snake."

My lips tighten. "Great metaphor, asshole."

"How does Xander put up with you?" he mutters under his breath. I reach over and pinch him.

"Ow! That was my nipple."

I shrug. "You should like that. I heard you like it rough."

He parks the car and stares at me wide-eyed. "Since when are you so mouthy?"

"I don't know. All I know is I'm a little more comfortable in my own skin nowadays."

I think I have Xander to thank for it.

Zach smiles at me and shakes his head.

"What?"

"Nothing."

"Tell me."

"No."

I open the car door and stand, cake plate firmly held in my arms. Zach gets the other two cakes out, balancing them on each hand.

"You ready for this, Trill?"

"Ready as I'll ever be," I say, turning to him. "Surely, nothing will go on today. It's an old lady's birthday party, not a weekend party with the women of Channon."

Zach chuckles. "Just wait until everyone starts drinking."

I open the door for Zach, since he has his hands full, and step in behind him. He takes me to the kitchen, which has three women getting stuff ready. They stare at me as I put down the cake.

"New piece?" one of them asks Zach.

He puts both cakes down and wraps an arm around me. "This is Trillian. Trill this is Mia, Veronica, and Sarah."

"Nice to meet you," I say, smiling at each of the women.

Two smile back at me, one doesn't.

"Where's Dad?" Zach asks them.

"Outside, grilling," the one named Mia replies. "Trillian, you the girl who lives next door to Grim?"

I nod. "Yes, that would be me."

"Come on, Trill. Let's get this over with," Zach murmurs, taking my hand and leading me to the back door.

"Get what over with?"

"My dad."

"It's not that much of a big deal, is it?" I ask, looking around.

"Me bringing you here is making you part of the club, Trill. Before you were family to us, but an outsider to the club."

He opens the door for me.

"What the fuck are you doing here, my Trillian girl?" is bellowed as soon as I step into the backyard, which is filled by bikers and their women.

I look up at Grim, who is standing on the opposite side of the lawn, tongs in his hand, and barbecue behind him.

All eyes are suddenly on me.

I lift my hand in an awkward wave as Zach leads me across the lawn to where Grim is standing. A few men, who were sitting stand and walk over to us.

"What are you doing here?" he asks me, scowling.

"I brought the cakes," I reply. "And I wanted to come for the barbecue. You say I'm family, then don't invite me to these events and I wanted to come. So I made Zach bring me."

I know I'm completely naïve to the whole MC lifestyle, and Zach and Grim only let me see what they want me to see. But like I said, they're family to me, and

I'd like to be more included and a barbecue seems innocent enough, right?

Two men stand behind him. One is young, and extremely good looking with jet-black hair and emerald green eyes. The other, slightly older, is a bulky man with blond hair and brown eyes.

"Where the fuck you been hiding her?" the dark-haired man asks, checking me out from head to toe.

Zach pulls me closer to him. "This is Rex and Snake."

Rex takes a step forward, grinning. "I call shotgun."

Grim slaps him on the back of the head, and the blond man, Snake, chuckles.

"This is Trillian. You fuckers don't get to go near her, you hear me?" He raises his voice. "No one fuckin' touches this girl."

Okaaaaay then.

I step closer to Grim, stand on my tiptoes, and kiss him on the cheek. "You going to feed me, old man?"

His lip twitches and then he turns to his son. "You let her come here in those fuckin' shorts?"

CHAPTER TWELVE

TRILLIAN

"You baked this cake?" Rex asks, licking his lips and staring right at me.

"I did," I reply warily.

"Talented," he murmurs, licking cream off his finger.

"For fuck's sake, leave her alone," Zach growls as he takes the chair next to me on the opposite side of Rex.

Rex puts his plate down on the table and scowls at Zack. "I'm just talking to her, or would you rather her sit here alone while you disappeared?"

"I didn't disappear. I was taking a piss if you must know," Zach fires back, then turns to me. "You okay?"

"I'm fine," I tell him honestly. And I am. Sure, a few of the men are very forward, and a little rough around the edges—okay, a lot rough, but they don't cross any lines. Some of the women are a little wary, whereas others are very friendly. I keep to myself and speak when I'm spoken to. Grim introduced me to everyone like a proud father, muttering threats to any man who stared at me too long or showed a little interest. We all sat around and ate together in the backyard, and I listened to them all talk and watched them interact. They really are like one, big, unusual family.

"So, this wasn't as wild as I was expecting," I say to Zach, so only he could hear.

He laughs, loudly. "Wait until tonight when all the old ladies leave."

"What happens then?" I ask, but I can guess.

He strokes the stubble on his face. "I get to have some fun, is what happens."

"You're dropping me home first, right?" I ask, saying each word slowly and deliberately.

He grins. "Why, you don't want to stay and play? Forget about Xander?"

"I'll make you forget anyone you want to," Rex inserts as his eyes linger on my breasts.

I roll my eyes. "Maybe another time."

Two men join us at the table, men I've never seen before. One has brown hair and eyes that match, a beard, and a gruff expression. But he's hot. Like holy hell hot. Wow. The man next to him is also a looker, in a completely different way—blond hair, blue eyes, and a friendly smile. He also has two facial piercings, an eyebrow ring and lip ring. He smirks in my direction.

"Hello there, beautiful."

"Off-limits, Rake," Zach instantly says. "Don't worry, there will be more pussy coming soon."

I elbow Zach in the gut, but he just grins. "Pig."

"Oh, come on, I wasn't talking about you."

The bearded man looks at me. "You his old lady?"

A 'fuck no' leaves my lips.

The men all laugh.

Zach puts a hand on his heart. "Don't be like that, Trillian."

"What's your name?" I ask.

"Arrow," he replies.

"Why do they call you—"

"Trust me, Trill, you don't want to know," Zach says, cutting me off.

Arrow grins then, and it brightens up his whole face. Damn. He really was something.

Rake's phone beeps and he checks it, then scowls. "My sister sent me a photo."

"Why the fuck are you scowling then?" Arrow asks.

Rake shows Arrow the photo and his eyes widen. "Fuck."

Rake quickly moves the phone from his sight. "She's too fuckin' beautiful for her own good."

His eyes then find me. "Kind of like you."

I can feel my cheeks heat from the compliment. This man really was a charmer.

"Still not going to fuck her, Rake," Zach says in a dry tone.

"But I want her," Rake says, eyes on me.

Wow.

"Get in line," Rex adds.

Shit, I forgot he was even there.

Zach half laughs, half makes a choking sound.

Arrow smirks. "You'll want someone else in an hour, brother."

Rake nods. "True."

These men were crazy—a mix of charming and complete assholes.

"Everyone loves the cakes," Zach says to me, changing the subject. "I think the ladies are going to come to you for every damn function now."

I smile. "That's okay, I don't mind."

And I don't.

CHAPTER THIRTEEN

XANDER

"How's she doing?" Persephone asks me, leaning on the side of the doorframe. I'm sitting in Summer's living room watching TV and thinking about Trillian.

"She's okay," I say. "I think she realises that sometimes bad shit happens without reason, and it's something she's going to have to move on from."

"That was our niece," she says quietly. Persephone is Ryan and Reid's sister and Summer's sister-in-law. When we first met, we hooked up a few times until I found out she was working at a strip club and hiding it from me. We fucked a few times casually after that, but she knows I would never consider anything more permanent. It just wouldn't work out for us. I liked her, but I didn't love her.

"I know," I reply, sighing. "It kills me to see the sadness on her face and watching her blame herself for something that wasn't in her control."

Persephone walks into the room and sits down next to me. "She'll be okay. Reid's looking after her."

I nod. "I know."

She puts her hand on my face and turns my head to her. When she moves to kiss me, I pull my face away. "Sephie, I can't."

She sits back and frowns. "Why?"

"Because I met someone and I don't want to screw things up with her," I tell her, wanting to be honest but not wanting to hurt her feelings.

"You met someone?" she asks, sounding shocked. "Who?"

"It's not that unlikely," I murmur at her astonishment. "A girl I met when I was visiting a friend. Remember, I told you I was going to a town called Channon?"

She nods. "So you were there for a couple of days max, and you already think she's the one?"

I scowl at the disbelief in her tone. "I think she's someone worth exploring things with, yes."

"Well, fuck me," she mutters under her breath, sagging back against the black leather couch.

My lip twitches. "Pretty sure we just discussed that *that* wasn't going to happen anymore, Sephie."

She sighs. "Guess I'll have to find a new fuck buddy, now."

"I guess you will."

We're both lost in our thoughts after that until she finally stands. "Going to be hard to replace you, Xander. No one fucks like you."

I burst out in laughter. "Good to know."

She walks out but turns back to me as she reaches the door. "Xander?"

"Yes."

"She's a lucky woman."

I smile, but she's wrong. It's me who is the lucky one.

*****

The next evening, I stare at Trillian's number on my phone, but don't press the green button. I know she deserves an explanation from me. I called her a few times, but she was usually busy with work and school. I stayed with Summer for a few nights before going back to my own house. Back where I started and nothing has really changed. I miss my dad, Summer still isn't herself, and what I really want is to be with Trillian. It seems like nothing is going right. I've been working a lot at my bike shop keeping the business going and checking in on Summer. I want to go back to Channon, but how long could I stay before I have to leave again? I'd called Zach a few times, and he promised me Trill is fine and he's looking after her, like he always does, he pointed out.

She doesn't even need me, does she?

I thought she'd be calling me every day, like my exes did, but she's been silent. She's fiercely independent and I like that, but I also miss the hell out of her.

Pressing the button, I put my phone to my ear, but it rings out, and then goes to voicemail. It's seven in the evening, and I have no idea where she could be. I decide to call Zach.

He answers on the third ring. "Xander, we were just talking about you."

"Who was?"

"Trillian and I. How you been, bro?"

"Good, so she's with you," I murmur, wishing it was me with her instead. "She didn't answer her phone."

"Yeah, she's a little preoccupied right now," he replies, sounding amused.

I hear loud music and laughter in the background. "Where are you?"

"Wind Dragons clubhouse."

My fingers squeeze the phone. "You took Trillian to your fuckin' clubhouse?"

"What?" he replies casually. "She wanted to go. I think she was lonely."

My free hand turns to a fist. "What is she doing?"

"Playing a drinking game with the women."

I curse. "She doesn't normally drink much."

"I know," he replies, chuckling. "She's decided to let go for once. Don't worry. I'm keeping a close eye on her and batting all the men away who are trying to paw at her. Let me tell you, it's a full-time job."

I see red. "Zach, I swear to God!"

"Guess I'll be seeing you soon, then, hmm?"

He hangs up on me.

That bastard.

What was he thinking by taking her there? I've heard the stories. The place is like a fuckin' brothel. I throw the phone down on the couch and run my hands through my hair, tugging on the ends. Standing up, I head to my room and grab a bag.

Zach's right.

He will be seeing me soon.

I decide to get a good night's sleep and then ride to Channon in the morning. It's six p.m. when I get there. I park my bike on Trillian's driveway and walk up to knock. She doesn't come to the door. Her car is parked in the driveway so I know she's home. Maybe she's in the shower. I take quick steps to Zach's front door and knock on there instead. He opens the door a few seconds later, wearing nothing but a pair of boxer shorts. He grins when he sees me, and I feel like putting my fist through his face.

"Where is she?" I demand.

He smirks. "Hello to you, too, Xander."

I push into his house and glance around.

"Please, do come in," Zach mocks from behind me.

I hear voices in the living room so I go there, then freeze as I spot her. She's sitting on the couch wearing a white dress and looking comfortable. On the other side of the couch is a man I've never met before. A biker. He's wearing the Wind Dragons cut and his eyes are on Trillian.

"Who the fuck is this?" I grit out, staring daggers at the stranger trying to poach my motherfucking property.

Fuck, this woman is making me crazy.

"I'm Rex, who the fuck are you?" the guy calls out cockily.

Trillian stands up. "Xander? What are you doing here?"

What am I doing here?

I look down at this Rex guy and feel nothing but pure unadulterated fury. "I came here to see you, but you're obviously fuckin' busy so I must have wasted a trip."

Her pouty, pretty mouth opens slightly. "I wasn't doing anything wrong."

Zach walks into the room and takes in the situation. "Rex is my friend. Yes, he wants to fuck her but he hasn't and won't. Trill only sees him as a friend, who she met like, yesterday. Now that that's all sorted out are we going out or what?"

No one speaks.

Zach groans. "Come on, Rex. Let these two sort their shit out."

"I'm here if you need me, Trill," Rex says.

His comment has me seeing red. If Trill wasn't sitting there looking beautiful as hell, I'd teach that fucker a lesson about staying away from what's mine.

Rex and Zach exit the room, and I have to physically stop myself from taking him down.

He wants her.

But he isn't going to fuckin' have her.

Trillian sits back on the couch and watches me, waiting patiently for me to speak. I sit down opposite her before I do.

"You didn't call. And I rang you yesterday and you didn't answer, only to find out you were at the clubhouse," I say, looking down at my hands.

Her eyes widen. "I didn't want to call and annoy you, Xander. I know you were dealing with things back home. It wasn't like you called me every day, and I didn't expect you to. You said you would come back, and I was waiting for you."

"Yeah, I can see how you were waiting," I scoff. "Why didn't you call me back yesterday?"

Fuck, I sound like a pussy.

She frowns. "When I got back from the clubhouse, I was exhausted and fell straight asleep."

"Trillian," I grit out.

"What?"

"Come here," I demand. "Now."

She glares at me, but she stands and steps in front of me.

"Straddle my lap," I tell her, my gaze not leaving hers.

She hesitates but then does as she's told, straddling my waist, our clothing the only thing between my dick and her pussy. I cup her face with one hand and run my other through her black, inky locks. She looks like fuckin' Snow White with her perfect red lips and clear skin.

"I missed you," I whisper against her mouth.

"I missed you, too," she replies, shifting on my lap, causing me to moan. "But I'm angry at you."

"I know, babe," I say quietly. "Let me make it up to you. Show you how much I need you right now."

"I need you, too," she whispers back.

"Prove it."

She kisses me, and I kiss her back, showing her how much I've missed her. I kiss her like this is the last taste of her I'll ever have, almost desperate, filled with need. I run my hand up her thigh, lifting her dress with it, loving the feel of her smooth, silky skin.

"We're leaving, just in case you wanted to know!" I hear Zach call out. "Not that it seems like you care!"

I hear the door slam shut and smile against her sweet lips. Reluctantly pulling my mouth from hers, I grip the hem of her dress and lift it up. She puts her hands up so I can easily slide it off her. She's left in a white bra and white lace panties.

"Who were you wearing this for?" I ask gruffly, my cock swelling to the point of pain.

"Shut up," she growls. "Just stop talking and fuck me, Xander. I need you."

Well, that was unexpected.

Her comment snaps the last of my control, and I fuse my mouth back to hers and take off her bra, throwing it somewhere on the floor. Then, I stand with her in my arms and lower to my knees, laying her out on the floor, not able to wait another second. Drawing back, I slide down her panties, my mouth watering at the sight it bears.

Fuck, I am suddenly very fuckin' hungry.

CHAPTER FOURTEEN

TRILLIAN

Xander glances up at me before spreading my legs wide and lowering his head. I've only had a guy go down on me once, but I don't think this is going to be like that time. The hungry look in his hazel eyes is so intense I feel like I could come from that alone. His pink tongue peeks out as he tastes me.

Fuck.

He's good at what he does. My hips arch as the sensations become too little and too much at the same time. He licks my clit and a whimpering sound escapes my lips. I had no idea it could be like this—that I could feel like this. I don't care right now that we are in Zach's house. I want him and I don't want to wait. I've waited long enough.

"Xander," I breathe, lifting my hips to his mouth. He lifts his head, eyes on me, and wipes his mouth. I realise he's fully dressed. "Take your clothes off."

I don't know where my sudden boldness comes from, but I just want him. He makes me feel beautiful, wanted, and accepted, and that makes me feel comfortable. Makes me let go.

He pulls his shirt over his head instantly and undoes the button on his jeans. I take him in greedily, his impressive build, toned muscles and artistic tattoos.

He's stunning.

Perfect.

He sits to the side to pull his jeans off, and then braces himself over me, fully naked. He lowers his head to my breast, licking around the nipple before sucking on it, and then does the same to the other. He starts kissing up my neck.

"Are you on the pill, Trillian?"

I shake my head.

"Fuck," he whispers, then sits up and grabs his jeans, pulling out his wallet and a condom that's in it.

I raise my eyebrow, but he just flashes me a boyish grin.

"I was hopeful."

He rips the condom open with a flash of his straight white teeth and rolls it on his very impressive length. He's huge. Beautiful. Long, thick, and smooth.

Positioning himself, he slides in gently until he's fully inside me. I feel full, wonderfully so, and when he pumps his hips, my breath hitches.

It feels amazing.

I pull him down, licking at his lips until he loses control and pins my arms above my head. Thrusting inside me, he kisses my mouth as I reach closer and closer. Then, it hits me, and I come—screaming his name, my eyelids fluttering as wave after wave of pleasure hits me. Xander gently bites down on my neck and then licks the spot with his tongue. I hear him curse under his breath, his breathing becoming erratic, his thrusts coming faster, quicker. His mouth descends on mine as he comes, his hands cupping my face.

"Fuck, Trill," he says, kissing me sweetly before pulling away and staring down at me. "Are you okay?"

I nod. "That was amazing."

His eyes are so soft and gentle on mine that, for a moment, I just stare up at him, enjoying the moment. "I can't believe I took you on the floor for our first time."

I grin, feeling sleepy and sated. "I don't mind. We can have sex on the floor whenever you like."

With him, I didn't care about the details. I just needed and wanted him.

He leans down and nuzzles my neck. "Let's go back to your house. I want you in your bed, in the shower, on your couch…"

I giggle, my fingers running down his muscular back. "Let's go before Zach suddenly decides to come home, or even worse, Grim walks in."

That would be extremely embarrassing.

Xander nods, kisses me once more, and then leaves to clean up in the bathroom. I dress, leaving my panties in my hand. When Xander walks out of the bathroom, he wraps an arm around my waist, the other around my nape, leaning me backward, kissing me like you'd see in an old movie.

Then, hand in hand, we walk to my house and get to know each other even more thoroughly.

"So, she lost the baby?" I ask, my heart breaking for his sister.

He speaks into the darkness of my room. "Yeah. She's doing a lot better now."

"I'm sorry," I tell him. "I can't imagine having to deal with something like that."

He kisses the top of my head, which is resting on his chest, our legs intertwined.

"I couldn't stop thinking about you," he says. "I didn't know what was going on in that head of yours and it was driving me crazy. And that wasn't exactly a conversation I wanted to have over the phone."

"I know what you mean," I reply quietly. "I'm glad you came back. I wasn't sure if you would. In fact, Zach said he'd take me to see you and I was considering it. But I didn't know where we stood and if you'd want me to come."

"I always want you to come, Trillian."

I grin at the double entendre. "I know that now."

His chest shakes as he chuckles. He's kept his word, making love to me on my bed, in the shower, on my couch and even on the back porch. I am exhausted, a little sore, and happy.

Deliriously happy.

I don't know what Xander and I are going to do, but I do know that I don't want him to leave. I think that we can work this out. I've never felt this way before, and now that I have found this with him, I want to keep it.

"Trill?"

"Yeah?"

"Sleep, babe," he commands gently. "I know you're tired."

I yawn and nuzzle his chest. "Night, Xander."

"Night, beautiful," he says quietly, kissing behind my ear.

I sleep like a baby.

*****

"Was it everything you dreamed about?" Zach asks the next morning, standing in my kitchen in his boxer shorts.

"You couldn't even get dressed this morning?" I ask him, making a face.

"No time," he says after a sip of coffee. "I need to know the gossip."

"Seriously? Badass biker by night, gossiping neighbour by day."

He chuckles. "Only for you, Trill."

I hide my grin and lift my own mug to my lips. "It was perfect."

Zach grins and leans forward against the counter top. "Where is he now, anyway?"

"In the shower."

"And you aren't joining him? That's just bad form, Trill."

"If you want to know, I'm a little sore, you know, down there, so I thought it would be best if I didn't join him because if I did, I'd be up against the tiled wall right now screaming his name."

I enjoy watching him spit out the mouthful of his coffee. "You know, Trill, anyone else says anything and I don't even flinch. Every time it comes out of your mouth, I'm caught off guard. Jesus! A little warning maybe? Xander must be good if he fucked the prude right out of you."

I pick up an apple from the fruit bowl and throw it at his head. He ducks and laughs as it hits the wall.

"Oh, come on, I'm just playing with you."

"You're a jerk!"

"You love me."

I shake my head at him. "You came over for breakfast, didn't you? I think the gossip was only second on your agenda."

He sighs, shoulders dropping. "I am very hungry."

I laugh, turning to the stove. "Okay, I'll make some pancakes, how about that? Or do you want waffles with strawberries."

"Waffles. Always waffles."

Xander walks into the kitchen, wearing jeans and a fitted black t-shirt.

"Zach," he says, nodding.

"Xander, you look well rested."

I roll my eyes and pull out the waffle maker. Xander comes up behind me, pushing my hair to one side, and kisses my neck.

"You want some help?"

"No, I'm okay. You can take a seat with our uninvited guest over there," I tease, sticking my tongue out at Zach.

"Oh, come on," Zach says. "After I let you fuck in my house and everything."

Xander walks over to Zach and slaps him on the back of his head. Zach laughs and playfully grabs Xander in a headlock.

I keep myself busy, turning away so Zach can't see my flushed face. I am never going to live this down with him. I just know it.

But it's worth it, so I don't care.

I make the waffle batter from scratch, stirring the mixture.

"You sure you don't want help?" Xander asks, watching my movements.

"You could wash and cut up the strawberries if you like."

"Make me look bad, why don't you," Zach says, smirking. "This is a whole new side of you, Xander."

"Shut up," Xander and I call out at the same time.

"Oh, wow, you even talk at the same time now," Zach chuckles. "And both ganging up on me. I see how it's going to be from now on."

Xander shakes his head at Zach. "You're a pain in the ass, you know that?"

I finish making the waffles and serve them with the strawberries Xander cut for me and some whipped cream. We all sit at the table, making jokes and enjoying each other's company.

It feels good.

After breakfast, Zach leaves the house, walking back to his own in his boxer shorts, and then Xander and I clean up. Xander insists on giving me a ride to uni, and then tells me he will pick me up when I'm done. He kisses me properly before he rides away, leaving my body tingling and his taste in my mouth.

I could get used to this.

CHAPTER FIFTEEN

TRILLIAN

The weekend comes around and I tell April I'll come out to Drake's to see her at work. I also think Xander might want to go out, even if it's just for a little while. I lick my lips when he walks out of my bedroom dressed for the night in dark jeans and a black shirt. His eyes roam over me, taking me in from head to toe.

"You look beautiful," he says, stepping to me and wrapping a possessive arm around my waist. He grips the blood red material of my dress and draws me closer for a kiss. The dress is one I've never worn before. Strapless, it hits above my knees and is cut out around my waist, showing a dash of skin. I've paired it with my strappy white shoes with a platform heel.

"You look amazing yourself," I tell him when he pulls back from the kiss.

"I almost want to drag you back into the room," he murmurs, hands squeezing my ass.

I roll my eyes. "You can pull the dress off after we go out for a little while. I promised April and I haven't seen her much this week."

"I wouldn't mind dancing with you again."

I smile at the memory. "I wouldn't mind that either."

We arrive at Drake's and head for the bar.

"Hey, April," I say, leaning over the bar to kiss her on the cheek. Xander stands behind me and pulls down my dress. I turn my head to see him staring at my ass and roll my eyes.

"April," Xander says, nodding at her and offering her a small smile.

"You both came," April says happily, bouncing on her feet. "What can I get you?"

I order an energy drink and Xander gets a beer. April slides the drinks over to us but refuses to take any money.

"You can't do that," I whisper-yell at her.

"I just did," she smirks. "Everyone does it all the time, calm down."

I open the can of my drink and take a sip, silently disapproving of her actions.

She ignores my scowl.

"I feel like I haven't seen you in so long. Good to see that you finally came out of your sex coma."

I smirk. "Sex coma? Is that even a thing?"

She shrugs, a smile playing on her pink lips. "I made it up, but it's still a thing. You know, your little sex bubble. At the start of a relationship all you want to do is tear off each other's clothes."

That's the truth, but now I'm feeling a little guilty over it.

"How about we catch up tomorrow?"

Her eyes brighten. "Yes, please. Come to my house, I'll cook you lunch."

"Sounds good."

The bar gets busy and April smiles apologetically. "You two enjoy. I'll be back."

She leaves to serve the customers and Xander takes the opportunity to slide me onto his lap. "Don't get angry," he says in my ear.

"Why would I get angry?" I ask with brows furrowing.

He grimaces a little before nodding his head in the direction of the dance floor. I turn to look and see Paulina, Xander's past conquest. She sees Xander and quickly heads in our direction.

I turn to Xander and scowl. "This is your baggage."

"I know," he mumbles. "I'll handle it."

"Hello, Xander, you're back in town," Paulina purrs. She glances down at me and scrunches her nose. "I'm surprised you're with her, considering she's Zach's."

I throw her a dirty look. It's she who's been with Zach before, not me. I know people around Channon think that I am with Zach, but they don't know the truth of our friendship. I don't really care what they say about us anyway, but I don't miss the way Xander's body stiffens at the mention of me being Zach's.

"She's not Zach's," he grits out between clenched teeth. "She's mine."

Paulina sniffs. "Well, if you want another taste of something better, you know where to find me."

Xander laughs without humour. "My woman is sitting right here and you think it's okay to run your mouth like that? I regret ever sticking my dick in you. Trust me. I won't be back for another anything."

Wow.

I think that's a little harsh, but keep my mouth shut tight. Like I said, this is his baggage, his to deal with.

"Fuck you," Paulina growls before she storms off, stomping away.

Xander kisses my nape. "Sorry about that. Don't let her ruin our night, Trill."

I puff out a breath, glad for the distraction when April returns. "Who was that?"

"A friend of Xander's," I reply, sliding off his lap and facing April. It really sucks to think about Xander with another woman, but I know he isn't a saint. I can't exactly be angry over this. I knew they slept together and I still wanted him. But damn if seeing her again didn't suck.

Xander takes my hand. "Let's dance."

I say bye to April and follow his lead to the dance floor. Facing each other, we dance, our bodies touching. Xander grips my waist and presses me against him. Kissing my lips once, he moves to my ear and kisses the spot just underneath it. "I don't want anyone else but you, Trillian. I don't even *think* about anyone but you."

He says the words loudly in my ear, so I can hear them over the music. I smile at him and reach up to kiss him back. The song mixes into another, one a little more upbeat than the other. Xander's hands run down my stomach, resting on my hips. I can feel his hardness pressing into my stomach, letting me know how much he wants me. It's a powerful feeling to have a man like this want you. It's addictive, all consuming, and I'm not sure how I'll deal when it's gone. We dance for two more songs then head back to the bar to get some water.

"Do you know how sexy you are when you dance?" he asks, grinning at me playfully. "The way you move your hips is… fuck."

I laugh at the expression on his face. "Are you kidding me? I think you're the only guy that can dance in the whole of Channon. Everyone was staring at me with envy."

I excuse myself and head to the bathroom. I'm in a stall, handling my business when I hear two women talking.

"Did you see her? She's fat. Why the fuck is he with her?"

Paulina.

"Who knows, maybe he likes them big."

They both laugh.

I know I'm not skinny, but I'm also not fat. My body is curvy, but not soft. It's just the figure I was born to have. The girls leave as I open the door and step to the sink, washing my hands and looking at my reflection in the mirror.

Don't let them get to you, Trillian. Xander wants you. They're just jealous.

I push all thoughts away, dry my hands, and exit the bathroom, and then I join Xander at one of the tables.

He stands up as he sees me and kisses my mouth gently. "What's wrong?"

"Nothing, why?" I reply instantly. I thought my expression was blank when I left the bathroom.

"Trill," he growls into my ear. "You look upset. Tell me. Now."

I sigh. "It was nothing. Just some girls saying shit about me."

He looks back toward the bathroom where I just came from. "Who?"

"Who do you think," I grumble. "It doesn't matter."

"Tell me what they said. I don't like anyone talking badly about you and I'm fuckin' pissed right now."

Great, now I have to relive it.

"They were wondering why you were with someone as fat as me," I say, cringing.

Xander lifts my face up so I can't look away. "Are you fuckin' kidding me? You're perfect. I love every inch of your body and I like that you're not stick thin. They're clearly just jealous."

I shrug. "I'm okay with my body. I exercise and I'm healthy. This is just my shape."

"I know, Trill. I love your body. I get hard just thinking about it so don't pay them any mind, all right?"

I nod. "Yeah, okay."

"Good girl. Do you want something else to drink?"

"No, thanks, I'm okay."

He cups the back of my neck and raises his head, looking behind me. "Who the fuck is that guy staring at you?"

I turn to look in his line of sight and cringe when I see Cain, the guy I lost my virginity to. He was my first and only boyfriend and the relationship lasted three years.

"Old friend of yours?" Xander asks, examining my face closely.

"You could say that," I reply, shrugging sheepishly.

"Come on, let's go."

Xander looks back at Cain then leads me outside the bar.

"What?" I ask as we walk up to his bike.

"I didn't like the way he was looking at you and last thing I need is to get into a fuckin' fight tonight."

My mouth drops open. "How was he looking at me?"

"Like he'd already had you."

He can tell that by one look?

"I had to deal with the same thing tonight from Paulina. And your time with her was much more recent, but you don't see me losing my temper," I say, crossing my arms over my chest.

"When did you sleep with him?" he asks, a muscle ticking in his jaw.

I sigh. "The last time was when I was eighteen. It was about three years ago. He just happens to live in the same town so I'm stuck seeing him around from time to time."

"He was your first?" he asks through clenched teeth.

"He was," I say slowly, nodding.

Xander takes a shaky breath. "Yeah, we're definitely getting out of here."

I roll my eyes. "Double standards, much?"

He draws me to him with a hand on my ass. "I don't think I've ever felt possessive of a woman before, and I don't exactly know how to handle it, okay? Right now, all I want to do is shove my fist through his smug looking face for having touched you at all."

I rest my hand on the centre of his chest. "You're overreacting, you know that, right? It's not like I saw you, spoke to you, felt a connection between us then went ahead and slept with someone else."

He flinches. "Ahh, come on, you can't throw that in my face, Trill. The difference is, you obviously felt something for this guy to give him your virginity. Everyone before you, I've fucked without emotion. Paula whatever the fuck her name is, I fucked her thinking about you. It could have been any woman there. It didn't matter. You were the only woman I wanted."

My eyes widen at his admission. I didn't want to think about him sleeping with anyone else whether he was thinking of me or not. In fact, I didn't know how to process that bit of information.

I inhale and exhale deeply then decide to change the subject. "Can we talk about this later? Where do you want to go now?"

"We can get something to eat and go back to your house," he says, tucking my hair behind my ear. "First we'll go and say goodbye to April."

"You sure you don't want to go anywhere else? I don't want you to have a boring time while you're here," I say. "I know we don't have much to offer compared to the city, but we still have a few fun places to visit."

"Babe," he says, grinning. "I came back here this time for you. I just want to be with you. I don't care what we're doing. Vertical, horizontal... I just want to be where you are."

My breath hitches. "Screw the food, we're going home. To bed. Now."

I step closer to his bike, and Xander starts chuckling. "Let's say bye to April first."

I pull his face down for a hungry kiss, showing him just how badly I want him right now.

"Fuck, Trill," he groans. "You can't kiss me like that in public. Do you have any idea how badly I want you? So bad it hurts. I don't think I'll ever stop wanting you."

What does one say to that? Instead, I kiss him again.

Then I go and say goodbye to April.

Then we ride home. I unlock the door and let us inside.

We don't even make it to the bed.

CHAPTER SIXTEEN

XANDER

ONE MONTH LATER

I know I can't stay here forever. I have to go back. I have my friends, my family, and my business that are all being neglected, and it isn't fair on them. While Trillian is at work or school, I help fix things around the house for her or I hang out with Zach. I also pay the bills even though we fought about it more than once, but that is something I won't budge on. I'm living here, so I'm paying, there's nothing else to say.

"You gonna stay in Channon now, boy?" Grim asks, sitting back with a beer in one hand and a cigarette in the other.

I sit back on the outdoor chair in Zach's backyard and strum my fingers. "I honestly don't know what I'm going to do. I could always get someone else to run Dad's shop, and I could go and see Summer and Mum every month, but it's a big decision, you know?"

Grim nods. "It is a big decision. You know you have us here, too. Wind Dragons are looking for new recruits if you're interested. I think you'd be an asset to the club."

He's mentioned this to me before. I rub my lower lip with my index finger, considering. My dad had been in an MC when he was younger. He somehow got out when he was fighting to get visitation with my sister, but still remained friends with his club brethren. I don't know how that worked out, but I heard him telling someone that he had to do something for them to get out.

"What exactly does joining the MC entail?" I ask, wondering if I want to take this route.

Grim chuckles, which turns into a cough. "You want me to give away our secrets before you join?"

I lean back in the chair. "Is the club clean?"

"We don't do anything illegal," he replies, smirking. "Well, that's a lie, but nothing too bad."

"Good to know," I reply dryly.

"If you move here, what are you gonna do about work? The club owns A & B Mechanics. You could work there. You would have passed it just as you drove into town. It's one of the legit businesses."

"I would still get the profits from Dad's shop even if I lived here," I say, running my hand over my hair in contemplation. "But I'd need something to do with my time. I don't like being idle. I've already fixed up everything in Trill's house and worked on her car. I was thinking of buying her a bike and doing it up for her next."

Grim whistles. "That serious, huh?"

I turn my face to look away. "That serious."

"She's a special girl," he muses. "Rex is practically panting after her."

My jaw tightens. "Don't remind me."

Grim grins and blows out smoke from his cigarette. "Let me know what you wanna do. You know I'll always take care of you, any way I can."

I nod. "I appreciate it. When's Zach getting his ass home?"

"He's probably getting fucked sideways back at the clubhouse."

I shake my head. "Have you seen Zach around Trill? He's like a whole different person."

"He's protective of her. She's like a sister to him."

"There's something about her that brings out my protective side as well. She's just so sweet, you know? How often do you come across a genuinely good person like her? Especially one that looks like her."

"Not very often," Grim replies, smiling fondly. "She's a good kid. Was very close to her dad, kind of like you were."

He glances at me, as his smile turns sad. "Messed up both of you to lose them so soon."

"At least I have Mum, you know? She didn't even have that," I murmur. "Did you ever see her mother?"

Grim shakes his head. "We moved in a couple years after her mother left. Heard she was a bitch though. Beautiful, but lazy. Entitled."

"Nothing like Trillian, then," I comment, knowing she's the opposite of all those things.

"Ian did a good job raising Trill. He loved her to pieces and raised her right. She wasn't spoiled or anything."

The back sliding door opens and Zach walks out. "There you guys are."

He's wearing his leather cut over a white t-shirt and dark jeans. "Want to go for a ride, Xander? I have business to take care of about an hour away from here."

Grim stares down his son. "You still didn't take care of that?"

Zach scowls. "Doing it today."

I stand up. "Trill's got classes until five, so I'm free."

"Sweet," Zach replies. "Let's get going, then. It's been a while since I've had a good, long ride."

"Heard you were having one just before you came here," I smirk.

Zach turns back, a grin playing on his lips. "Hey, I can always bring some of the club girls around if you're interested."

When I had a girl like Trillian? No fucking thank you.

"Think I'll pass on that one. I still have the last girl you set me up with causing problems," I admit.

Zach stills. "No shit? Did she say something to hurt Trill?"

"Just rubbing shit in her face, reminding her that we fucked that night."

Like we need that reminder.

"Oh, and she called Trill fat. Her and her friends were saying shit about her and Trill heard. "

"Jealous bitch. Fuck," Zach mutters under his breath. "I'll have a word with her. She should know better than to mouth off at Trill."

My chest tightens at the thought of someone other than me looking after and standing up for Trillian. "I'll handle it."

She should have gotten the hint from our last confrontation, but you never know.

We walk outside to the driveway, get on our bikes, and enjoy the ride.

*****

"What the fuck is he doing here?" I ask as I see Rex leaning against the wall of the building we stop at.

Zach's lips tighten. "He's a good guy. Don't hate him just because he wants to fuck Trillian. You'd have to hate half of the fuckin' town then."

This is true. However, I never said I was acting rational. I just keep seeing them both sitting there on that couch, like they do it every day, and I don't like it one bit.

We walk up to Rex, who smirks when he sees me, making me want to punch him in the face that little bit extra.

"What are we doing here?" I ask, having a bad feeling about this.

Zach cracks his knuckles. "Just dropping in for a little visit. You can wait out here if you like, Xander."

He and Rex walk into the building, a dodgy looking apartment complex, and I follow behind. We walk up a flight of stairs and then stop at room number twenty-four.

"Who lives here?" I ask.

"Someone who owes us money," he replies, stepping back and kicking the door open with one smooth movement.

Looks like they need better security here.

A bulky man walks out of the bedroom and pales when his eyes land on us. Zach closes the door behind us and walks over to the man. "We want what we're owed. You have twenty-four hours."

The man swallows and nods. "Yes, of course."

Rex grins cruelly. "Just as an incentive…"

He brings his fist up and punches the man square in the face. I hear a crunching sound and cringe.

"Fuck! Okay! You will have it by tomorrow, I swear!"

I exit the room before anyone else. If I had known this was some intimidation mission, I would have stayed my ass back in Channon waiting for Trillian to get home. I've been in trouble before. Hell, the first time my sister Summer met me, I'd just walked out of jail after spending a night in there for fighting. That feels like a long time ago, although it's actually just a few years. I have no plans to get in any kind of trouble again, which is why I've made up my mind that I don't want to join the Wind Dragons MC, although sometimes the lifestyle is a tempting one. Zach walks out with me but leaves Rex in the room with the man.

"What does he owe you?" I ask curiously.

"Cash."

"Are we bullying anyone else or we going back home now?" I ask dryly, pulling out a piece of gum and shoving it in my mouth.

"Home? Is Channon home for you now?" he asks, flashing me a knowing grin. "Am I going to need a suit one of these days?"

I put the chewing gum wrapper in my jean pocket and stare at Zach drolly. "Who knows? Maybe one day."

Zach chuckles. "Never thought I'd see the fucking day."

"What is Rex doing?"

"Scaring the shit out of that guy. We need him scared or he won't pay up. Instead, he'll call his friends up and have them start trouble with us."

I put my hand up. "I don't wanna fuckin' know any more."

Zach's lips twitch. "Does that mean you aren't going to become a prospect one of these days?"

"And be your little bitch boy? No fuckin' thank you," I reply in a dry tone.

Zach slaps his hand on my back. "You don't need to be in the MC. You're still like a brother to me, you know that."

"Well, next time please leave me at home for your little meetings like this one."

"Ah, come on, Xander. Enjoy the fresh air. The screams for mercy," he says, trying not to laugh.

I still and turn to stare him in the eye. "You're a sick fuck, you know that?"

He squeezes my shoulder, grinning and returns to his bike.

Note to self—avoid going on trips with Zach.

CHAPTER SEVENTEEN

TRILLIAN

I come home after my run to find Xander in the kitchen, bare-chested, cooking something on the stove.

"Smells good," I comment, placing my pink iPod down on the counter. I walk up behind him and wrap my arms around his narrow hips. "Pancakes?"

"Mmm hmm. How was your run?" he asks, turning around and enfolding me in his arms. I feel safe there. Protected.

"Good. Are you going to the gym today?" I ask.

Xander nods. "I will be. Listen, we need to talk about what's going to happen when I go home sometime this week. I've been back here over a month and I've got shit I need to take care of."

"I know," I reply, my shoulders drooping. "I'm surprised you stayed this long."

"Hey," he says, running his finger down my cheek, "it's not like I live in another country."

"I know," I whisper, pouting. "It's selfish of me to expect you to stay here. I know your life isn't here."

He turns and switches the stove off, then lifts me in his arms and sits me on the countertop. "Do you want to eat first or have a shower with me first?"

"Do you even have to ask?" I reply as I pull off my tank top and sports bra.

Xander's pink tongue peeks out to taste one of my nipples.

"I'm all sweaty," I complain, moving away from him.

"Don't fuckin' care, you always taste so good," he says, eyes on my breasts. Lifting me back into his arms, he walks to the bathroom and sits me down next to the sink. While he turns on the shower, I jump down and pull off my black yoga pants, socks, and shoes, then slide back up again. Xander tests the water temperature then slips down his boxer shorts, exposing his long, hard cock. I always want to sigh. I don't think I'll ever get tired of the view.

Xander kisses the spot underneath my ear then carries me into the shower under the spray of water. Grabbing a handful of my lime body wash, he puts me down and washes my body, inch by inch. When his fingers slide over my nipples, my breath hitches. When his hands wander lower, I press my back against the cold tiles and let him explore. His mouth finds mine while his fingers continue to do their magic. Just before I'm about to come, Xander lifts me up against the tiles and slides into me in one smooth thrust.

"So good," he moans, pumping his hips in a sensual rhythm that has me panting. My hands bury in his hair, pulling gently as my mouth works against his. I went on the pill two weeks ago and it feels so good having him inside me without a condom, no barrier between us. I trail my lips down his jaw, open-mouthed kisses down his neck, causing him to moan and thrust harder and faster. Xander reaches down to play with my clit in quick, smooth strokes that soon send me over the edge.

"Baby, I'm coming," he grits out.

"Me, too," I pant, clinging on to his body for dear life.

"Look at me, Trillian," he commands, eyes boring into mine as we both orgasm. "So fuckin' beautiful. Nothing is better than this, nothing. With you, everything is perfect."

He rests his forehead on mine as we both come back to ourselves.

"I love you," I whisper, being brave and saying the words for the first time.

Xander lifts his head, eyes flaring. "Say that again."

"I love you."

"Fuck. I love you, too, Trillian," he whispers back. "I want to love you, worship you, and ruin you in the best and worst way."

Then his mouth is on mine again.

*****

Life is short and you only get to live it once, right?

That's why I decide to go back with Xander for a week. My boss gave me time off work and I'll have to catch up on my uni classes when I get home. I emailed them saying I was sick and wouldn't be able to attend all week. Zach is going to keep an eye on my house and water my plants, so I'm all set. I'm excited to see where Xander lives and to meet his friends and family. I can't even remember the last time I left Channon. I think it was a few months before my dad died.

How depressing is that?

I talked Xander into taking my car for the drive so I can actually bring some luggage with us. He isn't happy to leave his bike behind, but he agreed.

"Are you ready to go, Trill?" he asks, loading the car with our bags.

"Yep," I call out, opening the passenger door and sliding in. Xander gets into the driver's seat and glances over at me.

"You look happy."

"I am happy. I can't remember the last time I went on a road trip," I tell him, doing a little happy dance that consists of a lot of fist pumping.

Xander's laugh travels throughout the car. "You realise it's mainly bush we're driving through?"

I roll my eyes and reach out to cup his jaw. "I don't care. It's going to be fun."

"Let's hope there are no kangaroos on the roads," he murmurs.

"As long as there's daylight, we should be fine."

"As long as I don't get distracted by those damn shorts, we'll be fine," he replies, starting the car and turning down the road.

I look down at my shorts. "What's with these shorts? Zach made similar comments when I wore them to the clubhouse."

I watch as Xander squeezes the steering wheel, his knuckles turning white. "You wore those to the clubhouse? Fuck, no wonder half the men are in love with you."

I roll my eyes at him. "That's an exaggeration. I think they just liked my skills in the kitchen."

"I've sampled your skills in the kitchen," he replies in a low tone, reaching his hand out and resting it on my thigh.

"I know you have," I reply, grinning, "but you haven't sampled my skills in a car, yet."

His head snaps to me. "Are you trying to get us killed?"

I shake my head. "No, but I believe there are a few stops on the way where we could park for a little while."

I stare at his handsome profile as he laughs. "I've created a monster."

"You have no idea."

I want him in the worst way, always. I can't get enough. I'm addicted to him. I feel like I've changed as a person for the better, like I've come out of my shell and started living life more, instead of just reading about it.

"I like that you can be open with me, say whatever crosses your mind," he says, squeezing my thigh.

"I trust you," I tell him, "so I feel comfortable around you."

He takes my hand in his and brings it to his mouth, kissing my knuckles. "I'll never break that trust, Trillian. It's a gift."

I sigh contentedly. "And that's why I trust you."

He rests our intertwined hands on his thigh. "I can't wait for you to meet everyone. Summer is going to love you."

I hope so.

"Can we stop for some beef jerky?" I ask Xander, turning my body and leaning my head on his shoulder.

He chuckles. "We can stop for anything you want."

He's so good to me.

"Let me know when you get tired so I can drive," I tell him, not expecting him to drive the whole ten hours by himself.

"Let me know if you want to stop at a hotel on the way. We don't have to do the whole drive in one go," he says.

"I can manage, you don't have to baby me," I tell him, turning the volume up when an Ed Sheeran song starts to play on the radio.

"I'm not babying you," he replies, grinning. "I just want you to be comfortable."

He's spoiling me.

And I'm getting used to it.

*****

"Why didn't you wake me?" I ask as we pull into his driveway. "You let me sleep the whole way while you drove!"

"Don't be angry. You looked so cute sleeping. So peaceful. I couldn't wake you. Besides, I wasn't tired, I'm fine. It wouldn't be very manly of me to let you drive while I sleep in the car."

I open my mouth and then close it. "You're so damn stubborn sometimes!"

"Come on," he says. "You can yell at me more once we get inside the house."

His voice sounds amused.

Amused!

Opening the car door, I slide out and stretch. We stopped about four times, for toilet and food breaks. I got my beef jerky, and I loved it. Now, what I really want is a hot shower and a decent meal. Xander carries our bags then sets them at the front door while he pulls out his keys. The house is an older one, but nice and well maintained. Xander opens the door for me and I step inside before him, glancing around the house eagerly. It's modern inside. I love it. It isn't cluttered at all. Instead, it's spacious and tastefully decorated.

"It's beautiful," I tell him, turning to face him. He smiles, putting our bags on the floor, and then stands in front of me with a playful expression on his face.

"You're beautiful. Do you want to have a shower? I'll order in some food for tonight. Then tomorrow we can go grocery shopping. Summer's been keeping the house clean and checking in. I'm not sure just how stocked the fridge is, though."

I nod. "Sounds good. Are you going to join me in the shower?"

He lowers his head and kisses my mouth, just the barest of touches. "I'll join you. Come on, I'll give you a quick tour of the house."

He shows me the bedrooms, bathrooms, kitchen, and living area. Walking me back to the first bathroom, he leads me inside and starts to strip off my clothes—first my t-shirt and shorts and then my bra and panties. I turn the shower on and look back at him to see his eyes lingering on my body.

"Like something you see?" I purr, sinking my teeth into my bottom lip.

"I like everything I see," he replies in a husky tone. I step under the water and crook my finger for him to join me.

He removes his clothes, opens the glass door, and steps into the shower. "Can't believe you're in my house right now."

I reach down and take his cock in my hand, stroking gently. "Well, you better believe it. I'm all yours for the next week."

Xander squirts soap into his palm and washes the both of us. He washes my hair, his fingers on my scalp make my toes curl. Once I rinse, I lower myself to my knees and stare up at him. His hazel eyes are dark and his cock twitches in front of me. I stroke him once more with my hand as I lick the head, twirling my tongue around it. He moans and puts one hand on the wall, the other coming down to rest on my head. I take as much of him as I can into my mouth, hollowing my cheeks and sucking him in deep.

"Fuck, Trill," he groans as he gently moving his hips.

I continue to suck him, just how I read in one of my romance novels. I did this once or twice to Cain, but I didn't like it. Cain had grabbed my hair and was a little rough with me, which I didn't like one bit. Xander, on the other hand, waits patiently, his hand in my hair, gentle instead of demanding. I could taste him all day.

"I'm going to come if you don't stop, Trill," he tells me, his tone pleading. He gently tries to push my head off him, but I don't let him. Instead, I suck him harder and use my hands at the base of his cock as well as my mouth.

"Trillian," he whispers.

He comes in my mouth, spurt by spurt and I swallow every drop. When his body stops jerking, I hold onto his thighs and slowly remove my mouth.

"Holy fucking shit," he says in a ragged tone, leaning his head back against the tiled wall. "That was amazing, Trill. I don't think I've ever come that hard in my life. Seeing you on your knees like that. Fuckin' fantasy."

He helps me up and turns the water off. Grabbing a white fluffy towel from the rack, he unfolds it and wraps me in it, drying me. After he dries my body, I wrap my hair in the towel while he gets out another one and dries himself. Silently, he leads me into his room, drops his towel, and sits me on the end of his bed. When he lowers to his knees and spreads my thighs, I fall back on the bed, my pulse racing.

"Xander?"

"What?" he whispers. "You didn't think I'd leave you wanting, did you? I'm going to make you come with my mouth, then with my cock. Then I'm going to feed you, and then, Trillian, we're going to sleep in my bed. Naked and wrapped in each other's arms."

That sounds perfect.

Then his mouth is on me… and it is perfect.

CHAPTER EIGHTEEN

TRILLIAN

Summer is beautiful, an absolute stunner.

"Nice to meet you, Trillian," she says, pulling me in for a hug.

"Nice to meet you, too," I reply, smiling. "I've heard so much about you."

Summer takes a seat on his couch and we do the same. "Better be all good things."

Xander wraps an arm around my waist, bringing me closer to him. "Mostly. Where's Reid?"

Summer sips from her glass of water then puts it back on the coffee table. "He's at the gym with Ryan and Tee."

"Who's Tee?" I ask Xander.

"Some crazy-ass woman Reid teaches self-defence to," Xander replies, shaking his head. "You've heard of the band Morning Alliance, right?"

I nod, my eyes going wide and glazed. Of course, I've heard of them.

I fucking love them.

Xander sighs. "Tee is Saxon's woman."

"Holy crap, seriously?" I whisper, my hand coming up to my mouth. "Wow."

Summer laughs. "I know, right. He's sexy as hell."

Xander's eyes narrow on me.

I shrug and my lip twitches. "I didn't say it, she did."

"But you were thinking it," Summer adds, smirking. "Calm down, Xander. The woman is yours, but she isn't dead. Saxon Tate is a looker."

Xander scowls. "We're kind of friends with him. Hang around in the same circle."

Summer laughs and nods. "Yeah, he comes into the bar from time to time."

"No effing way," I mutter. I have to meet him. Have to. The whole band. "Maybe you could send me a text or something next time they're going to be there."

Summer laughs harder.

Xander scowls harder.

I look between the two of them and decide to change the subject. "So, Xander says we're going out to the bar that you and your husband own tonight?"

The one the members of Morning Alliance apparently frequent.

Holy crap.

Summer nods, a grin playing on her lips. "Nice change of subject. And yes. Knox's Tavern is Reid and Ryan's bar. I think you'll like it."

She turns to her brother. "What are you guys up to for the rest of the day?"

Xander runs his fingers across my collarbone. "I have to go in to work. Trillian wants to see the shop so I'm taking her with me. Then we will meet you at the bar tonight."

Summer gives me a gentle look. "You two seem happy."

"We are," Xander replies quietly, his eyes on me and a smile on his mouth.

"Dad would have liked her," Summer adds, smiling sadly and wringing her hands.

I watch Xander for his reaction. His eyes turn pained for a second, but then he squeezes my hand. "He definitely would have."

I look down. "I hope so."

I know my dad would have liked Xander, too. Well, as much as a father can like a man who's sleeping with his baby girl.

"I hope we can spend some time together before you leave, Trillian," Summer says. "Get my number from Xander. You can call me anytime, okay?"

That was really sweet.

"Thanks," I reply. "I'd like that."

She smiles at me then looks at her watch. "Shoot, I have to get going. I'll see the two of you tonight, though."

We say our goodbyes, and Xander and I walk her out. When the door closes, he turns to me and touches my chin with his fingers. "You okay?"

I nod. "She's lovely."

He smiles fondly. "She is something, that's for sure. Do you want to hang out a bit or go straight to the shop?"

I open my mouth to answer, but there's a knock at the door.

"Summer must have forgotten something," he murmurs, opening the door. But it isn't Summer. It's a pretty little blonde staring up at Xander with a smile on her face.

"Heard you were back. Sick of life in the country?" she asks, stepping over the threshold. She turns her head and finally sees me standing there.

"Oh, hi," she says, tucking her hair behind her ear.

I look at Xander, who clears his throat, looking uncomfortable. "Trillian, this is Persephone, a friend of mine. Sephie, this is Trill."

Sephie? He's never mentioned her before. But they've been together at some point. I know it. I can tell by their body language. And the way Xander is acting confirms it. The air between the three of us thickens to the point where I take a step back.

"Nice to meet you, Persephone," I finally say.

She smiles at me then looks up at Xander. "Sorry, I didn't know you had company."

"Trill's staying with me for a week," he says, staring at her pointedly.

This is getting awkward.

Well, even more awkward.

"Should we go into the lounge room?" I ask, looking between the two of them. I begin to walk past Xander, who pulls me against his body.

"Oh, um, actually, I think I might get going," Persephone says after Xander flashes her a look.

"Will we see you out tonight?" he asks, running his fingers up my spine.

She glances at me before replying. "Not sure. Maybe. Was nice meeting you, Trillian."

"Bye, Sephie," Xander says, closing the door as she leaves.

I turn and walk into the kitchen, pulling out a drink from the fridge just to give me something to do.

"She's Reid and Ryan's sister," he says suddenly.

I close the fridge and stare him down. "And an ex of yours?"

He licks his lips, looking away. "We've been together in the past, yes."

"And why did she come here today? What would have happened if I wasn't here?"

Would he have slept with her? And I would be back in Channon without a clue. The thought occurs to me. "Did you sleep with her last time you were here?"

Xander walks over to me and cups my face in his hands. "I haven't touched another woman since Paula or whatever her name was that night. And I didn't even kiss her! I wouldn't cheat on you, Trillian. I'm many things, but disloyal isn't one of them."

I exhale slowly. "So if I weren't here, what would you have done? And be honest."

"I would have spoken with her. We're friends at the end of the day. Then she would have left. I wouldn't have touched her in any way," he tells me, eyes gazing into mine. "I promise you, Trill."

"She's beautiful."

"So are you. More so. And you're mine, so that makes you everything to me."

"Why didn't you want her to come inside? It made it feel like you were hiding something from me," I say quietly.

He looks away. "I didn't want to hurt you, Trillian. It was awkward for me. I knew it would upset you. Fuck, I saw that guy you'd slept with and I wanted to kill him. You've already had to deal with that other woman, now I didn't want you to have to deal with Sephie as well."

Just how close is he with her?

Am I overthinking this?

"Okay?" he asks, kissing my brow.

I sigh. "Okay."

I said that I trusted him. Now I need to prove it. To myself.

*****

Knox's Tavern is completely packed. I meet Reid, Summer's husband, Tag, Dash, and Ryan and his wife Taiya. They all seem so nice, and I can tell they are all really close. Xander has a great group of friends. Persephone is absent. I watch Xander interact with his friends, laughing and joking. He always makes sure to include me in conversations, or ask if I'm okay or if I need anything. He's very attentive, and I appreciate that.

"Have I told you how sexy you look tonight?" he whispers in my ear, running his hand down my bare back.

"Only about ten times," I reply, my cheeks heating. I'm wearing a black backless dress with long sleeves and a high neckline. The back is the focal point of the dress, of course, showing everything from my neck to just above the dimples on my lower back. I let my curly hair run wild, curls framing my face and draping over my shoulders. I put a little eyeliner around my blue eyes to make them pop, a little pink gloss, and I'm good to go.

"You're distracting me," he murmurs. "I don't even want to talk to anyone. I just want to take you home and do dirty, dirty things to you."

"Xander," I giggle. "We have to stay at least another hour. You haven't seen these people in a month. You need to socialise."

He buries his face in my hair. "I know."

"Xander, let the woman go for one second," Tag mutters, smirking. "She isn't going to run off."

Xander ignores him and kisses me instead.

"Okay, Xander, seriously," Summer interrupts. "I'm going to dance with Trillian. You go and have a drink with the guys."

She grabs my hand and pulls me to the dance floor. "Never seen my brother behave this way. In fact, if someone told me he was, I wouldn't believe it."

I don't know what to say to her, so I just give her a small smile.

She takes me to the centre of the small dance floor and starts to move to the music. After a little while, I relax and do the same. I notice the men never approach Summer or get too close to her. I wonder if that has anything to do with Reid and the fact that he's a trained mixed martial arts fighter. When I feel a pair of hands on my hips, I know instantly that it isn't Xander. I push the hands off me, turn, and shake my head. The man before me grins charmingly and shrugs in a 'well, I had to try' kind of way. Unable to stop myself, I grin back. Unfortunately for me, he takes this as a yes and takes my wrist, pulling me into him.

"I'm sorry, I'm taken," I tell him. "I'm not interested."

Instead of being deterred, he decides to grope my ass.

Before I know what's happening, I'm pushed behind Xander, who says something to the guy. The man then pushes Xander, whose body doesn't even falter, instead standing still and strong. Just how strong is Xander? Horrified, I watch as Xander raises his right arm and punches the man right in the jaw. The man staggers back, cupping his jaw. Xander takes another step toward him. Suddenly, I'm grabbed and pulled away from the commotion. I look back to see Reid with his arms around my waist and my back pressed to his chest. He carries me like I weigh nothing.

"Stay here," he demands, putting me safely behind the bar, right next to Summer. Reid goes back to Xander, who just hit the man again.

"Holy shit," I mutter, not knowing what the hell to do right now.

I look at Summer, who is staring at her brother wide-eyed. "Whoa."

Whoa? That's all she has to stay?

"What the hell do I do?" I ask her.

"Stay here like Reid said. He will sort them out," she says, taking my hand in hers and squeezing gently. "I don't think I've ever seen my brother lose his temper like that."

She looks at me as if seeing me for the first time. "Don't hurt him, Trillian. He's got himself so worked up over you, I don't know if it's a good thing or a bad thing."

I don't know what to say to that.

I see Xander searching the crowd for me, then heading toward me. Jumping over the bar, he wraps me in his arms, crushing me to his body. "Are you okay?"

"I'm fine," I tell him. "You didn't have to hit him, Xander."

He shudders slightly as I rub his back. "He fuckin' grabbed you. No one gets to touch you, Trillian. You're mine and they should fuckin' know better, and now they will."

I bury my face in his chest, listening to his racing heart and ragged breaths. "Let's go home."

He nods and kisses the top of my head.

"Too beautiful for your own damn good," he rumbles into my ear.

Then he drags me out of the bar and takes me home.

CHAPTER NINETEEN

XANDER

I scared her.

I'm an idiot.

Trillian puts a bag of frozen peas on my knuckles, but I just watch her. I saw her face after I hit that guy, and she looked scared. I never want to see that look on her face again. When I saw him putting his hands on her, I lost it. I saw red. I don't think I've ever been that angry in my life. What's happening to me?

All I know is I didn't like seeing another man touch her. She's mine and that's final. At first, I told him to back off. I controlled myself. But when he pushed me first, all bets were off. I've never been so possessive of a woman before. I've never really cared that much if I'm honest with myself. Even with Sephie. After being with Trill, I realise that all Sephie and I had between us was an attraction that turned to friendship. There are always plenty of available women around, and one is just as good as another, but it's so different with Trillian. I'm fuckin' whipped, is what I am. The worst part is that I don't even care. She's worth it.

"Do you get into a lot of fights?" she asks, wrinkling her nose.

Great, now she thinks I'm some asshole who starts shit everywhere he goes.

"No, I hardly get into fights," I tell her. "I'm sorry if I scared you. I just saw you telling him no, but he still touched you and I lost it. I was trying to calm myself, but when he pushed me, he gave me the perfect excuse to teach him a lesson for touching you."

She runs her hand up my bicep, her eyes lifting to mine.

"I was a little scared," she admits. "More shocked, but shit happens, right? We're both okay and that's all that matters. You need to understand that I'm yours, and only yours."

If feels fuckin' good hearing her say those words.

"Is that right?" I murmur, lifting her onto my lap, straddling me.

She nods. "Trust me, if another woman touched you, I wouldn't like it one bit."

I gather her hair in my hand and move it to one side, over her shoulder. I lean forward and kiss her neck, my tongue licking the spot between her neck and shoulder. She shivers, so I do it again.

"I don't want to touch anyone but you," I whisper, my lips exploring her neck. "And I never will."

She threads her fingers through my hair and pulls my head back so our mouths are almost touching. "I love you."

"And thank fuck for that," I whisper against her pouty red lips. "I don't know what I'd do if you didn't."

Then I kiss her.

The kiss isn't polite or reserved.

No, it's hot, all consuming, and demanding.

It's hungry. It's needy.

It's teeth clashing, biting and sucking.

Licking.

Tasting.

I devour her mouth.

She moans as my hands start to wander over the dress I'd wanted to rip off her all night. Sliding the slinky black material up her thighs, I push the dress over her hips and up under her breasts.

"Arms up."

She lifts her arms and I pull the dress off. Underneath, she's braless, so she's left in nothing but a black thong. I cup the bare globes of her ass with both hands, squeezing and fondling. My mouth then pays attention to her breasts and sucks on her nipples.

"Shit. Xander," she groans as I playfully nip and lick. I do the same to the other, not wanting it to feel left out. Standing with her in my arms, I lower her to the floor. Reaching down, I rip off her thong in one swift move.

"Leave the heels on," I tell her, taking a step back and greedily taking in the sight before me.

Fuck.

I'm so hard and want in badly.

Her dark curly hair is wild and untamed, framing her pretty face and falling down her back. Her blue eyes are heavy-lidded, staring back at me with such desire and need that I want to fall to my knees. Her pink nipples are beaded, begging for more attention that I'm going to give her in due time. Her small waist flares out into wide hips that I love so much. My eyes lower to her pussy, bare except for one strip of trimmed hair, then down to her sexy, strong thighs. Last, I enjoy the view of her heels, making her legs look even sexier.

And she's all mine.

How did I get so lucky?

"Turn around," I tell her, my voice trembling slightly. "Put your hands on the wall and stick your ass out."

She nibbles on her bottom lip before doing as I asked. She places both hands flat on the wall, bending at the waist, sticking her ass out to me.

What a fuckin' view.

Her ass is perfectly rounded, and she has a lot to grab.

I like that.

A lot.

I pull off my shirt and remove my jeans, already having taken off my shoes when I entered the house. Sliding down on my knees behind her, I cup her and lower my mouth to her pussy. I start with one short lick before settling in for the long haul. Soon, I have her screaming, begging and pleading with me to let her come. When I feel her thighs tremble this time, I don't pull away. I keep my mouth on her clit as she comes, sliding a finger inside her. I drag it out for her as long as I can, then stand and slide into her with one smooth thrust. She curses. I grip her hips, take a few steps back, and sit back down on her bed with her still on my dick, her back to my front. Hands on her hips, I lift her up and down, bouncing. My mouth finds her neck and my hands move to cup her breasts. My hips work up and down, thrusting up into her. Fuck, I can't get enough. What has this woman done to me? She reaches her hands back and holds onto the back of my neck, then turns her face for a kiss. I slow down the rhythm of my thrusts as I pay attention to her lips.

I love these lips.

"You feel so good, Xander," she groans. "I never knew it could be like this."

I never knew it either.

When I feel myself on the edge, I reach down and play with her clit, wanting us to come at the same time.

My hand on her neck, we look into each other's eyes as we do.

*****

I don't know what I'm going to do. Am I going to move to Channon to be with Trillion? Can I go back and forth? That isn't exactly a permanent solution, but it seems smarter than committing to moving so soon. Trillian has two days left before I have to take her back, and I have no idea what to tell her. How long can I stay this time? I've been spending a lot of my time here at the shop, and Trillian either tags along or Summer takes her out somewhere. Those two seemed to have hit it off, and I know Summer genuinely likes Trillian, so that makes my life much easier.

"Mornin'" Trillian mumbles, eyes fluttering open and a sleepy smile spreading on her lips.

"Mornin', beautiful," I say quietly, rolling over and bringing her closer to me.

"What's wrong?" she asks, glancing up at my face.

I smile. "Nothing, was just thinking."

"About?"

"Making plans to come back to Channon. Wondering how I'm going to work it all out."

Her brows furrow. "I don't want you to give up your life. It's unfair to ask you to do that. Maybe after I finish uni, I could move here?"

My eyes widen. "You would do that? Leave your dad's house?"

She licks her bottom lip. "I wouldn't sell it, but I could rent it out or something."

I know how much the house means to her, so her offer is a big fuckin' deal.

I place a soft kiss on her forehead. "You have a year left of uni, right?"

She nods. "Yeah."

"Okay, so for now, why don't I keep going back and forth, and then we can work out the details later. If you're happier living in Channon, then that's where I want to be."

Her eyes turn heavy-lidded. "You're amazing, do you know that? Best man that I know."

I grin. "Just don't tell anyone else."

She rolls her eyes. "What are we doing today? What's the time?"

"Eight."

"Shit. I was going to go for a run." She throws me a playful look. "You're ruining my routine, Xander Kane."

I grin and lay on top of her, pulling her under me. "I think your routine needed to be shaken up a little. There's no fun in routine. You have to be spontaneous every now and again. Live a little."

Her look turns sultry. "I was spontaneous earlier this morning."

I harden at the memory. "Fuck, that was amazing."

I woke up at around four a.m. with Trill's mouth wrapped around my cock. Best way to wake up—ever.

She kisses my jaw. "I thought you'd like that."

"How about we go out for breakfast?" I suggest. "After I show you how much I enjoyed this morning, of course."

"What did you have in mind?" she asks, raising an eyebrow.

I grin and lift my hand to her hair, trying to push back her dark, wild curls. "I'm going to taste that sweet pussy of yours, and then I'm going to let you ride me so I can sit back and enjoy the view."

Her eyes flare and her mouth opens slightly at my demand.

But then she pulls the blanket down and spreads her legs in invitation.

Fuck.

I can't get enough of her.

I grab her waist and lift her so she's straddling my face.

CHAPTER TWENTY

TRILLIAN

Three nights later, we arrive back in Channon. Tired from the drive (even though Xander didn't let me drive, again) we both have a quick shower and practically fall into bed. The next morning, I wake up slowly, trying to force my eyes to open as I hear someone knocking on the door. Cursing to myself, thinking it must be Zach coming over to see us and demanding breakfast, I walk to the door still half asleep, dressed in my leopard print pyjama bottoms and tank top. I yawn as I undo the locks and open the door, sticking my head out.

"Zach, couldn't you have waited until…" I trail off, seeing that it isn't Zach at the door at all. Instead, a woman stands there. Dark hair and vaguely familiar.

"Trillian?" she asks, taking me in from head to toe.

"Yes," I reply. "I'm sorry, do I know you?"

The woman tightens her lips. "Of course, you know me. I'm your mother."

My eyes widen and my jaw drops. I examine her facial features. It's her. What's she doing here now? After all these years?

"What are you doing here?" I ask.

She scowls. "Is that any way to talk to your mother?"

My jaw tightens. "After you abandoned me when I was a child? I think I can talk to you any way I like."

Is it really her?

Dad kept one picture of her on the wall. One. It was of them at their wedding. I don't know why he kept it. If it were me, I would have burned the damn thing. I took it down when dad died and put one up of him and me instead.

She's aged, obviously. Her face is lined with wrinkles, but her eyes are the same. And her hair.

Fuck, it's her.

"Are you going to invite me in?" she asks stiffly, lifting her chin up at me.

It isn't the reunion I had always envisioned. In my dream, my mother runs to me and wraps me in her arms. She gives a good reason as to why she left and tells me how much she missed me. How beautiful I am to her. How she wants to make up for missed time.

I don't get any of that.

I feel… numb.

Blank.

"Trillian," I hear Xander call out from behind me, breaking me out of my stupor. I turn around to look at him as he walks to me in nothing but a pair of boxer shorts sitting low on those delicious hips of his.

"Who is it?" he asks, running his fingers through his messy brown hair. I want nothing more than to slam the door in my mother's face, forget it ever happened, and get back into bed with my sexy boyfriend.

So that's what I do.

I slam the door shut, lock it, and walk back to the bedroom, taking Xander's hand along the way.

"Who was it?" he asks again, staring at the door.

"No one," I mumble. "Just my mother."

Xander stops in his tracks. "What the fuck?"

I turn to face him and sigh as she starts pounding on the door. "It's my mother and I can't deal. She's a bitch. She wants something, I just know it. Why else would she be here?"

Xander scrubs his hand down his face and looks between the door and me. "We should at least find out what she has to say, right?"

I shrug. "I guess."

"Okay," he says, placing a hand on my arm. "Let her in. I'll throw some clothes on and meet you in the lounge room. You're not alone in this. I'm here, okay, Trill. And I won't let anything happen."

I believe him.

"Okay," I whisper.

He kisses my lips. "I'll just be a minute."

I nod, attempting a smile, and head back to the front door.

Time to face my past.

Xander is fuming mad.

And I mean fuming.

"You mean to tell me, after abandoning your husband and child, you're coming back here after all these years to claim that this house is yours and you want it back?" he says, disbelief filling his tone.

My mother sips the cup of coffee I made her. I should have laced it with something. "Your father and I never actually divorced. So, all of this should belong to me."

I'm speechless.

My mother is a cold-hearted bitch.

"Dad left this house to me in his will," I say. "It's mine. You left and you have no say anymore. Now, why don't you please leave, and go try to ruin someone else's life."

Her eyes darken. "If you want to go to court, then fine."

Xander laughs without humour. "I think if you had to come back here for this house, you don't have the money for a court case. I know a lawyer in Perth and I'm sure she would love to help us out in this situation. So, I guess we will see you in court. Now, get the fuck out of Trillian's house."

My mother stands up. "If I had known my own daughter would treat me this way, I never would have returned."

"You returned for the house, not me. Let's not pretend you're a good mother," I add.

I can't believe her audacity. Does the woman have no shame or pride? Xander walks her out while I sit and stare at the wall. I can't believe this. I'm so damn disappointed right now that it's not even funny. I hear the door close, and then I'm safe, wrapped in Xander's arms.

Only then do I allow the tears to fall.

Later that day, Zach paces up and down my kitchen. "I will handle this."

I put my orange juice down. "What are you going to do, threaten her?"

He grins evilly. "She doesn't know just how well-connected you are, does she? I'll just inform her. No one messes with one of our own and gets away with it. Wait until dad hears about this. Fuck, he's going to lose it."

Xander walks into the kitchen, back from the gym. "Hey, Zach."

He slaps him on the shoulder in an affectionate yet manly way.

"Hey, bro. Heard you met your future mother-in-law."

I can feel my face flush. Does he have to bring up something like marriage?

Xander chuckles. "Yeah, she was a real treat."

Zach runs his finger over his bottom lip. "I have a plan."

Xander looks instantly suspicious. "Let me guess, you're gonna threaten the shit out of her until she backs off and leaves Trillian alone."

Zach grins, his eyes taking on a devious gleam. "Yep. The bitch is gonna learn her place."

Xander looks to me, trying to judge my reaction. I just shrug, causing his lips to curve upwards. "I'm in. Anything to keep that woman away from Trillian. But if we have to go to court, I spoke to Tee, and she's on call for us if we need her.

Tee, as in Saxon from Morning Alliance's wife?

I try to keep myself from fan-girling.

And fail.

"Why do you have a creepy serial killer-ish look on your face?" Zach asks me, frowning.

Xander laughs, clutching his stomach. "Fuck, imagine if you actually met Saxon. You'd probably faint."

I puff out a breath, making a few of my curls wave in the air. "So, I like Morning Alliance, sue me."

Great choice of words, considering the situation.

Xander groans. "Yeah, you're never meeting any of them. I wouldn't want to be arrested for beating the shit out of them."

Zach makes some whipping sound effects.

"I'm going to have a shower," Xander says, wiping his forehead with his hand. He's wearing a pair of blue basketball shorts and a white t-shirt that is pasted against his body. He's in damn good shape, every inch of him toned and ripped. He pulls off his t-shirt, and I check out his chest and abs before moving to his arms. I love his arms. I stare at the sun tattoo he has, the one I know is meant for Summer.

"Just thought you'd like a closer view," he says, grinning and flexing.

Zach throws a tea towel at him. "You two make me nauseous."

I lick my lips, my eyes still on Xander. Then, making sure he's watching, I put my hands on the bottom of my top and move as if I'm going to pull it off.

"What the fuck," he grits out, quickly moving to me and hiding me from Zach's view.

"What?" I ask innocently. "I was just going to give you something to look at, too."

Zach groans. "I'm leaving. I can't take all this foreplay. I'm going to get laid."

We don't look away from each other as Zach leaves, slamming the door behind him.

"Okay, now you can pull that top off," he murmurs, flashing me a lopsided grin, "and those jeans, too."

I take two steps back from him, smiling playfully before I run to the bedroom, squealing as he chases me.

He catches me and throws me on the bed.

How I love this man.

CHAPTER TWENTY-ONE

TRILLIAN

Walking down the street, I stop to give some money to a homeless person.

"Thank you, miss," the man says gratefully as he takes the ten-dollar note from my hand.

I smile at him then continue walking along the busy shopping street. My mother wants to meet me for lunch. She called my mobile number, which I have no idea how she got in the first place. I didn't want to go at first, but then I realised I just want her to leave, and this is the only way for that to happen. Stepping into the restaurant, I look around until I see her sitting at a booth in the back. Exhaling slowly, I step in her direction, sitting down opposite when I reach her.

"Trillian," she says, her expression blank.

We order drinks before I get to the point of this lunch.

"What did you want to talk to me about?"

She purses her lips and glances around the restaurant. "I was paid a visit by your friends. How you have a motorcycle club behind you, I have no idea. Looks like Ian raised you to be trash."

My hands clench. "Don't you dare say anything bad about Dad. He was my hero and a million times the person you will ever be. I'm sure you don't want to upset me. It would be a shame if it reached Wind Dragons MC."

She swallows. "Keep the stupid house."

"Why did you want it anyway?" I ask, staring at her.

She seems to consider whether to tell me or not, but then shrugs and speaks. "My boyfriend left me and cut me off. He was filthy rich but didn't leave me with a cent. I was living with him, and now I have to find somewhere else to stay."

"If you were a nice person and needed a place to stay, of course, I would have offered the house to you," I say. "But you're not. I'm sure you can find some other man to mooch from."

She scoffs. "Listen to you, acting all high and mighty, but trust me, if you were in my shoes, you wouldn't have wanted to stick around, either. Your father was always working and I was stuck in the house with you twenty-four-seven. It would drive any woman crazy."

I roll my eyes. "Whatever you have to tell yourself. Dad and I managed just fine without you."

The drinks arrive, and I'm thankful for the interruption.

"Thank you," I say to the waitress, who bobs her head at me then leaves.

"What about his insurance money? Surely, you could give me a little of that."

My jaw drops. "Are you fucking serious right now? Is that why you really came here? Hoping to get a chunk of money?"

She narrows her eyes. "I know for a fact he had a large insurance policy. I know he took my name off it and gave you everything. I'm your mother at the end of the day, and I deserve some of that money. I was still his wife in name."

I stare at her for a few seconds and realise that she's dead serious. I finish my drink in three huge gulps, put some money down on the table, and walk out. She isn't getting a cent from me. She doesn't deserve it. She isn't my mother. She's a woman who gave birth to me. There's a difference in my eyes. If my dad wanted her to have something, he would have put her name in his will.

He didn't.

The fact that she didn't even come to my dad's funeral, but decided to come when she needs money, says everything I need to know about her. She isn't someone I want in my life.

She's toxic.

And I'm better off without her.

*****

"You should have let me come with you," Xander says for the second time.

"It was something I needed to do alone, you know? I faced her and now it's over."

He makes a sound in his throat and kisses the side of my neck. "I hope she leaves town now."

"Me, too," I reply, trying to ignore the pain over the person my mother turned out to be. A shit one.

"So, I was thinking," Xander murmurs, "I could do two weeks with you and two weeks back home. I could start working on cars too, to keep me busy while I'm here. What do you think?"

I don't like the sound of him leaving for two weeks every month, but the idea seems logical and reasonable. "I'm going to miss you."

He gently plays with my hair, resting his arm on the headboard of my bed. We're both naked and wrapped up in each other's arms. "I know. We could try it out and see how it goes. Nothing is set in stone. We can make it work for us."

"Okay," I reply, knowing what he says is the truth. We aren't in a rush. I can't even explain the overwhelming urge I have to be around him, an urge I'm sure is reciprocated. Well, he's here, isn't he? He's changed his whole life for me, and I never want him to leave. I meant what I said, if he wants me to move to Perth with him, I will. I would miss Channon, but I would miss him more, so it's a no-brainer for me.

"Are you happy here?" I ask, raising my face so our gazes connect.

He smiles gently. "I don't think I've been happier."

Then his lips are on mine, and my fingers are tangled in his hair.

And all is right in the world.

*****

It's Zach's birthday, so Xander and I are at the clubhouse. This party is a lot different from the other one I went to, mainly because of the women. There are more of them and they're wearing fewer clothes. I put down the massive chocolate cake on the table. It has a picture of a naked pin-up girl on it, since Zach is a perv and that's what he asked for. Xander is carrying two full trays of cupcakes and other treats I made for the occasion.

"I feel weird walking into a bikers' clubhouse holding cupcakes," Xander murmurs, chuckling to himself.

I smirk at him. "Zach has the biggest sweet tooth. Women and chocolate—that's how you get him."

A woman walks by wearing, I kid you not, pasties over her nipples and a skirt. I narrow my eyes on Xander to see if he's staring at her.

"You better not be staring at her tits."

He puts the trays down on the table and lifts his hands up in the air. "Come on, what do you want me to do? There're only so many places I can look, and there're women everywhere. You know I don't want anyone except you."

I know it, but I just want to annoy him a little. I didn't even see him looking at that woman.

Pursing my lips, I arch a brow at him. "Fine, but that means I get to look, too."

I see Rake walking towards me with a smile on his face. "Trillian without Zach—looks like I got lucky."

Xander steps next to me and pulls me in by the hips. "She's mine, so not so lucky."

Rake crosses his arms over his chest. "This dude? Not even a fuckin' biker? I'm disappointed in you, Trillian."

I smile because I can see the playfulness in Rake's eyes. "He rides a bad ass bike. He's just not in your MC."

The two of them start talking about bikes until Arrow walks up to us.

"Trillian," he says with a chin lift.

"Hey, Arrow," I say. "This is Xander."

"Trillian's taken," Rake says, sounding upset.

Arrow grunts. "I'm sure you'll find someone else to keep you occupied. We gotta go. Sin needs us."

Then they're off. Rake blows me a kiss as they depart.

"Want to tell me how you know bikers from other chapters?" he asks, frowning a little.

"Bikers seem to like me," I tease, batting my eyelashes at him.

He studies me for a moment before he lifts me in the air over his shoulder. A squeak escapes my lips as he slaps me on the ass and carries me outside where everyone is sitting and drinking.

"Put me down, Xander!" I laugh, pinching his tight ass.

He puts me down and takes a seat, pulling me onto his lap. "You don't want to look at anyone else, Trillian. All you can see is me."

Cocky bastard, but he's right.

Zach walks over and plops down in the chair next to ours. "Is April coming?"

I glance at him in suspicion. "Why?"

He shrugs, running his hands through his hair. "Just asking, Trillian."

"Is something going on between the two of you?" I blurt out. "Both of you are staying close-lipped about it."

A blonde sits down on Zach's lap and he points to her. "Does this look like something is going on between April and me?"

I grit my teeth. "You can be an asshole sometimes, Zach. You better not hurt April or I will personally kick your ass."

He sighs. "We hooked up, but we aren't together, all right? It was a one-time thing."

There is obviously more to the story, but I'm not going to pry. Whatever they're going through, I'll be there if one of them wants to talk about it. If not, then I'll try to mind my own business.

"Enjoy your birthday," I tell him. "You seem agitated. Just how much have you had to drink?"

He cups the blonde's breasts. "I am a little agitated. I know exactly what will take the edge off."

"Pig," I mutter.

"Let him be," Xander says in my ear. "He'll figure things out."

I turn my body so I can look at his face. "You seem sure about that."

"Xander knows me well," Zach says, chuckling. "We do everything together, you know. Or at least we used to."

"Zach," Xander snaps, glaring daggers at him.

"What exactly does that mean? It's not like I've stolen him. You guys still see each other," I say, thinking that Zach must be angry that Xander spends most of his time with me.

Zach groans. "So innocent, Trill. I meant that if you weren't here right now, Xander and I would be taking this sexy woman on my lap upstairs. Together."

"That's enough, Zach," Xander growls, standing up but not letting go of me. His fingers tighten on my waist.

Wait, what?

They've shared women before?

What the hell?

I try to push off Xander's hold on me, but it doesn't work. He just grips tighter. "It's in the past, Trill, let it go."

Let it go?

Let it go?

This isn't a fucking Disney movie.

He finally lets me go and I storm off. I hear Zach mutter a curse and I turn my head just in time to see Xander punch Zach in the gut, the blonde forgotten and standing in the corner.

Looks like Zach isn't having the best of birthdays.

I make it to the front, but then realise that Xander rode us here on his bike.

"You okay?" Rex asks, jogging over to me.

"I want to go home."

"I'll take you," he offers.

I know Xander will be angry, but right now, I don't care, I just want to leave.

I eye him warily. "You haven't been drinking?"

He shakes his head. "I just got here. I was at work. Come on."

I follow him to his bike and let him take me home.

CHAPTER TWENTY-TWO

XANDER

I punch Zach in the stomach, losing my temper. What the fuck is wrong with him? Why would he say something like that to Trillian?

"Fuck, I'm sorry," he grits out, holding his stomach. I look around to see one of his club brothers walking over to us, probably wondering why I'm hitting him on his birthday. In front of his club. Yeah, not the smartest thing I've ever done, but it looks like only one of them saw what happened anyway.

"Zach?" The man comes up, looking to Zach for instruction, probably on whether to kick my ass or not. Well, he can try.

Zach holds his hand up. "It's fine. I deserved that." He stands up and nods. "We better find her. I shouldn't have taken my shit out on her. I'm sorry. Fuck, I keep messing shit up."

"What's going on with you?" I ask, walking with him. "Fuck, do you have any idea how much shit you just put me in?"

He cringes because he knows it's bad. He knows Trillian. We were in such a good place. I don't need her head filled with insecurities because she has absolutely nothing to worry about with me.

"I fucked up, Xander. I'm sorry. Let me talk to her."

"Fuck, no," I snap. "I'm going to have to talk to her and explain that, yeah, when we were younger we did some shit, but I didn't even know her then so she can't exactly hold it against me. The worst thing I did was not tell her about it, but how do you start that conversation? Oh, did you know that Zach and I have had threesomes before?"

Zach makes a strangled sound. "Fuck, fuck, fuck. I wouldn't call it a threesome. It's not like we touched each other. We just shared a chick."

He shrugs, like it's no big deal.

"Zach, do me a favour and shut the fuck up. Trillian is going to think up all this shit in her head now," I say. "And she's going to trust me less."

We stand in the driveway just in time to see her leave on the back of Rex's bike.

"Motherfucker!" I yell, seeing red.

What is she thinking? Getting on the back of Rex's bike? She knows I don't like him. And this is the first time she's been on someone else's bike. I don't like it one bit. She's mine and she should know better.

Zach scowls. "He should know better. Everyone knows not to go near Trillian."

Yeah, that's true, but no one can say no to her.

"I'll see you later," I tell Zach, walking to my bike.

"I'm coming."

"You're drunk, you can't ride."

He sighs. "Fine, but I'm fuckin' sorry, all right. Today's been a shit day. No excuse, though."

I ignore him and straddle my bike.

I need to go get my woman.

*****

Rex's bike is nowhere in sight when I pull up in Trill's driveway. Maybe the man is smarter than he looks. Pulling out my key, I unlock the door and storm inside. I find her sitting in front of the TV. She doesn't look at me even though she has to have heard me enter.

"Will you listen to what I have to say?" I ask gently.

"Do you know what it feels like to find out something from other people that you should have heard from your boyfriend in the first place?" she fires back.

"That isn't really something I wanted to share with anyone."

Especially with her.

"Zach is one of my best friends, even though he was a dick tonight, and you and he have slept with the same women before? At the same time? Do you know how awkward that is?"

I sit down next to her but don't touch her yet. "Baby, it's not a recent thing. We were young, horny, and stupid. I hadn't even met you then. How can you hold it against me?"

She stares down at her hands. "When was the last time?"

I rack my brain. "I think we were twenty. So a few years now."

"I just feel like… What if you want to do something like that again? What if I can't keep your interest? You have all this sexual experience and I have hardly any. I don't want you to get bored," she admits in a small voice.

I lift her face so she has to look at me. "It didn't mean anything. I love you. I wouldn't change you for anything. Do you understand me? If I wanted that, I could have it, but I don't. We were young and experimenting. I know I should have told you, but to be honest, I didn't want to scare you off, and it's not something I just go around sharing. We haven't spoken in detail about my sexual past and I thought that maybe you didn't want to know."

She cringes. "I don't want to know details or anything. But if we run into someone you've been with, I'd like to know that."

I tilt my head to the side. "Okay, that I can do. You can ask me anything you want, Trillian. I've never lied to you."

"I know you've been around," she adds, sniffling, "so it's hard to believe sometimes that you're willing to settle down with me and be with only me."

I lower my head to taste her sweet lips. "I want you. Only you. I'm fuckin' obsessed with you, Trillian. We just are, you know? You're the one for me. Stop questioning it, baby. I love you."

"I love you, too," she whispers, her body relaxing. She leans her head on my shoulder, and I exhale slowly in relief.

"I just can't get the image out of my head," she whispers. "I know it's stupid."

"What you feel isn't stupid, Trill. It never is, not to me. I know I'd hate it if our places were reversed. The only thing I can say is that nothing that happened before matters anymore. This right here is what I want, and you are who I was meant to be with."

She flashes me a small smile. "So you don't want to share me with anyone else?"

"Even the thought of it makes me want to kill someone. If there's something you wanted to do or try, I will do it for you, but I'd never want to share you. Ever. I don't think I'd handle it very well."

"Understatement," she mumbles.

I kiss her temple. "You're mine and mine only. I'm greedy when it comes to you."

"Well, I'm glad," she replies in a dry tone, "because if Zach put his penis near me, I'd probably scream."

She's only joking, but the thought of Zach or anyone near her, makes me extremely angry.

"It's just you and me, Trill," I say, trying to calm myself. "We don't need anyone else or anything else to get us by."

"Just… I don't want to hear anything else from someone else. I'd like it to come from you, okay? When someone else tells me things, it makes me feel like I don't know you."

I've really fucked up.

"Okay, I promise," I tell her, meaning every word. "I'd never do anything to mess this up. I might be a dick sometimes, but I'd never cheat on you, or look elsewhere. Why would I? I'm not stupid or blind. I know the value of what I have in my arms."

"Xander—"

"Next time you get pissed, you don't fuckin' run away, Trill. Getting on Rex's bike? I didn't like that."

In fact, I hated it. I didn't trust that fucker, and I didn't like her being on his bike, especially because I know he wants her. I also wanted to make sure she was safe.

"I know," she says. "I'm sorry. I just wanted to leave."

I nod. "We're still learning about each other every day. We'll get there. We're going to make mistakes, but at the end of the day, we'll come together, just like this. But you need to talk to me. Don't run from me. I want you too fuckin' badly to ever let you go."

She giggles. "You're so smooth."

Liking the sound of her happy giggles, I push her back on the couch. "Smooth? Hmmmm. With you, it's just me being honest."

"And with the other women?" she asks, wrinkling her cute nose.

My mouth twitches. "Yeah, okay. I can be pretty smooth."

She bursts out laughing and I just watch her.

I could watch her all day.

CHAPTER TWENTY-THREE

TRILLIAN

ONE MONTH LATER

Leaving straight from uni, I meet April at a café.

"How was class?" she asks.

I shrug. "Same old crap. You?"

She shrugs. "Same."

We share a grin.

Xander is back in Perth and has been for the last week.

It sucks.

It sounds like a first world problem, but it really sucks. I miss him and want him back here. I miss him making me laugh, us sharing meals together, hugs.

The sex.

I *so* miss the sex.

But even more than that, I just miss *him*.

His presence. His warmth.

"Did you hear what I just said?" April asks, pursing her lips and staring me down.

I clear my throat. "I'm sorry, what?"

She sighs. "I just admitted that I slept with Zach and you weren't even listening."

I may have not been listening before, but I am now.

"I knew it!" I call out, standing up and clapping.

She grips my arm, trying not to laugh. "Sit down. People are staring at us."

I sit down.

"So what's the problem?" I ask, sipping on my milkshake.

She leans her chin on her elbow.

"He's a manwhore. It was just a one-time thing…." She trails off, wincing. "That happened once before when I was like eighteen."

My jaw drops. "Why am I only hearing about this now?"

She groans, covering her face with her hands. "He's your neighbour and friend. It was awkward."

"So you slept with him again? When?" I ask, frowning a little.

"The day before his birthday," she says. "He came into the bar and… shit might have happened."

So that's why he was in a shitty mood on his birthday? Something isn't adding up here.

"Are you sure it was a one-off thing?" I ask, trying to figure these two out.

She nods, playing with hair. "Yeah. He's amazing in bed, like wow."

Probably all the practice he's had over the years.

"So what now, then?" I ask, tilting my head to the side.

"Now, nothing," she replies nonchalantly. "We pretend it never happened."

I expel a sigh. "I don't get the two of you."

She picks up a forgotten fry on her plate and pops it into her mouth, chewing thoughtfully. "When does Xander get back?"

"Next week," I reply, allowing her to change the subject.

"You must be bored without him," she says. "You two are practically married."

"Are not."

"Are too."

"I do miss him," I admit. "The house is dead without him. I've gotten used to having him there and he kind of spoils me and I only realise now just how much."

April scoffs. "Brat."

I smile at her. "Are you finished eating?"

She throws her napkin down on her plate. "Yes, let's go shopping. I'm going to do some damage today."

We both stand and walk to my car. "Do you actually need anything?"

She glances at me, her blue eyes sparkling. "What kind of question is that? I need everything. New jeans, new shoes…"

I shake my head at her. "Let me guess. You're going to try everything on and take three hours in each store."

I never try anything on. I just buy it. I don't have the patience. April is the opposite. She'll spend all day in a store and enjoy every second. She'll also ask my opinion on every item she tries on. I usually make sure to bring snacks in my handbag to keep me occupied.

We get into the car and sing along to the songs playing on the radio. It feels good to be spending time with April. Really good.

But I also miss Xander.

A lot.

*****

"Wooo!" I yell, poking Zach in the chest. "I beat you again! How does it feel to lose to a woman?"

Zach shakes his head at my antics. "And such a good sport you are."

We're playing pool at the clubhouse. He apologized to me about what happened on his birthday. I know he was in a bad mood and it is really unlike him to take it out on me. He's never been anything but kind to me. Of course, I forgave him. He's like my brother. I'll always forgive him.

"I think this is the only thing I can beat you at, so yes, I'm going to milk it for all it's worth," I say, chalking up my pool cue.

A woman walks over and presses herself against him.

"I'm busy," he tells the woman, then looks at me. "Let's play again. If I win, you have to bake me whatever I want."

I see Grim walking over to us. When he reaches us, he leans down and kisses me on the forehead. "How's my girl, Trill?"

I smile widely. "Beating your son at pool."

Grim grunts. "What's fuckin' new? Zach, we're going on a run tonight. So don't be fuckin' going anywhere."

Zach nods at his dad and glances back at me. "Who's gonna keep an eye on Trill?"

I roll my eyes. "I'll be fine, don't worry about me."

Grim's eyes soften. "Someone will be staying behind to watch her, don't worry, but I need numbers tonight."

My eyebrows furrow. "Is everything okay?"

"Club business," both Zach and Grim reply at the same time.

Grim walks off and Zach strolls over to me and wraps an arm around my shoulders. "Xander's been calling me."

"And?"

"And he's going insane. And I might be working him up to amuse myself."

I narrow my eyes. "What do you mean?"

What's he saying to him? I can only imagine.

He chuckles. "Oh, come on, let me have my fun."

"Just remember that payback is a bitch," I mutter under my breath. He hasn't spoken to me about April. He never even mentions her and I have to wonder what's going on in that head of his.

"He's been calling me twice a day," I say. "It sucks being in the house without him, you know?"

Great, I've turned into one of those women who can't function without their man.

Zach kisses my cheek sloppily, making kissy noises. "Don't worry, he'll be back soon. Trust me. He thought he could do this two weeks on two weeks off thing, but this isn't some fly in and out job, this is his relationship with you. He doesn't want to be without you. He's probably sitting there imagining all the men trying to hit on you and it's slowly driving him crazy."

Or maybe Persephone is going over to keep him company.

I push that thought away. I know that he wouldn't cheat on me. I know. I trust him. But she could still go to his house for a friendly chat or whatever she wants to call it.

I wipe my cheek and glance at Zach as he runs his hands through his reddish brown hair. "You're a great guy, you know that, right?"

He raises an eyebrow at me, smirking. "What brought this on?"

I shrug. "If you and your dad hadn't been there for me… and then you brought Xander into my life. So thank you. I'm grateful to have you in my life, and one day, you will make a woman really happy. If you stop being a manwhore, of course."

He studies me. "April told you we slept together, didn't she?"

My jaw drops open. "What? What makes you say that?"

"I knew it!" he says, leaning back on the pool table. "It happened. It was amazing. And now she's avoiding me and pretending it never happened. I'll never understand women."

"Probably because you slept with her when she was eighteen and then moved straight on to the next," I say, blinking slowly.

"She told you that, too? Jesus Christ, what did you have? A 'bitch the shit out of Zach' day?"

I laugh at the expression of horror on his face. "No, she just mentioned it. Girl talk, you know? And I put two and two together and figured out that's why you were in such a shitty mood on your birthday."

"Are you trying to have girl talk with me, right now?" he asks, scratching the stubble on his jaw. "Because, yeah, I'm not doing that."

I throw my hands up in exasperation. "You like her. Just admit it!"

His eyes widen. "Where did that outburst come from?"

My lip twitches at that. "I know you do. I just want you to admit it."

He looks away from me. The coward. "I like a lot of women."

"You like her more."

"You're a pain in the ass, you know that?" he says with a small smile.

"But you love me anyway," I add.

"I do," he replies, "but that doesn't mean I want to have deep conversations with you where I bare my soul about things I'd rather not talk about."

"Fine, but whenever you're finished being stubborn, you know where to find me."

"Wherever Xander is?" he teases, laughing at his own joke.

"You're not funny."

"I'm hilarious," he says, nodding. "Now, are we going to play or talk about our feelings all evening?"

"We're going to play," I say, racking up the balls.

I beat him, of course.

But I baked him whatever he wanted anyway.

CHAPTER TWENTY-FOUR

TRILLIAN

He moves inside me slowly, teasing me.

"Xander," I plead.

"I missed you," he replies against my breast, licking one nipple and then the other before kissing up my neck, my jaw, and finally, my mouth. I thrust my hips upwards, silently begging for more. He's taking his time with me, drawing it out. I'm so wet that I can feel myself dripping.

"Missed you, too, Xander," I reply, my fingers digging into his taut ass and pushing him down into me.

Need more.

Harder.

Faster.

"Greedy," he murmurs. "You feel so good. I want this to last for-fucking-ever."

I suck on his neck, biting gently. He grinds his hips down into me, and his hands cup my face.

"Come for me, Trillian," he demands. "I want to feel you coming around my cock."

He increases his pace, finally giving me what I wanted from the beginning.

"Yes," I moan. "So good."

It doesn't take long for me to erupt. I clench around Xander, and soon, he's coming with me—our eyes and our souls connected.

"I love you," I say, barely a whisper.

"I love you, too," he whispers back. "That's why I'm not leaving again."

"What?" I ask, loudly this time. "What do you mean?"

He slides out of me, heads to the bathroom and returns with a cloth. After cleaning up, he sits against the headboard and looks down at me.

"I hated being there without you," he admits, looking a little sheepish. "It didn't feel like home anymore, you know? So I made a decision. I'm going to move here, permanently."

I sit up and straddle his lap, looking into his beautiful hazel eyes. "Are you sure that's what you want? I don't want you to regret anything."

"I'm sure," he says. "I would never regret anything to do with you, Trillian, never."

He's moving to Channon for me?

I reach down to my arm and pinch myself.

Ouch.

Yeah, it isn't a dream.

"Did you just pinch yourself?" he asks, chuckling softly.

"I can't believe this is happening," I reply. "I missed you so much when you were gone. I can't think of anything better than you staying, but what about your family and work?"

He puts his index finger against my mouth and I nip at it.

"I'll sort everything out. We can go and visit my family or they can come here. The business can be sorted out, too."

I rest my forehead on his shoulder. "I kind of love you."

"Good, because you're kind of stuck with me."

He kisses my lips, and I feel him getting hard again.

When he slides into me with one smooth, long thrust, a moan escapes my lips.

I could get used to this.

"Baby?"

"Yeah?"

"Marry me."

"What?" I ask, stopping my hips. "Xander…"

"Marry me, Trillian. I know it's soon and I know we're young, but I know what I want. I want you."

My breath hitches. He wants to marry me?

Do I want to marry him?

Fuck yes, I do. I want him.

There's no doubt in my mind at all.

"Say something," he pleads, hands running down my back. Gently sliding me off him, he goes to where his jeans are lying on the floor and pulls out a little black box. Crawling onto the bed, he opens the box and holds it out to me. The ring is stunning. Gold with a princess cut diamond. I love it.

"Of course, I'll marry you," I say, tears pooling in my eyes as he slides the ring onto my finger.

It fits perfectly.

Just like him.

*****

"All it took was one trip away from her, one, and you came back forever?" Zach says, slapping his thigh and laughing.

Xander just smirks and kisses my temple. "Laugh all you want. I get her, so I don't give a shit."

"It wasn't one trip, he went away before," I add, defending my man.

Zach shakes his head. "Yeah, but this was the new plan. Two weeks here two weeks there. One trip, that's it."

"Keep laughing, dickhead," Xander mutters. "Looks like we're going to be permanent neighbours."

Zach sobers, his eyes softening a little. "Trillian could do worse, bro. I'm glad it's you."

I smile, looking down. "I'm glad you say that, Zach because I have something to ask you."

"What?" he asks, standing straighter. "Is everything okay?"

"Everything is fine," I tell him. "I know it's unconventional, but I was wondering if you would walk me down the aisle."

I considered asking Grim, but Zach is the one who was always there for me, and he didn't have to be. He was my friend, my family and my protector for so long. I love the hell out of him.

His eyes pop from his head. "You're fuckin' getting married?"

He looks down at my hand and I flash my stunning ring.

"You two are fuckin' insane, you know that, right? Certifiably," he mutters, his face looking a little pale. "Married? You want me to walk you down the aisle? Fuck, I think that's the nicest thing anyone has ever asked me."

"Is that a yes?" I ask, batting my eyelashes.

Zach's expression softens on me, his pale blue eyes gentling. "Fuck. Anything for you, Trillian, you know that."

I step to him and he wraps me in his arms. "You deserve everything, Trill. All the happiness in the world."

I pull away from his embrace and lean up to kiss him on the cheek.

"Okay, that's enough," Xander says, only half joking, grabbing me by my hips and drawing me against him. "Keep your hands off my woman."

Zach and I share a smile.

Xander grins at Zach and claps him on his shoulder. "Thank you. For everything."

"I didn't do anything," Zach replies. "Always here for the two of you, you know that."

I watch as his eyes lower to my stomach. "No reason to rush the wedding, is there?"

I purse my lips. "I'm not pregnant. And the wedding isn't going to be rushed. I thought we'd wait a few years."

"Good," he replies, mouth twitching. "Just checking. Now, will you feed me? When you told me to come over, I thought I was just coming here for some food."

I roll my eyes.

And then I feed the two most important men in my life.

EPILOGUE

FIVE YEARS LATER

TRILLIAN

It's official.

I am going to swoon.

At my own wedding.

But not because of my husband.

"Nice to meet you, Trillian," Saxon Tate says, lifting my hand to his mouth and placing a kiss on it.

Holy fucking shit.

"Get your hands off my wife, Sax," Xander growls, walking up to me and pulling me to his side.

Xander got Morning Alliance to play at our wedding.

Morning Alliance.

At my wedding.

He's the best husband—ever.

In the world.

In the history of husbands.

God, how I love him.

"So how did Xander get someone as beautiful as you?" Ryder, the band's lead singer, asks.

I open my mouth, but nothing comes out.

Xander elbows Ryder in the stomach. Summer, standing next to me, laughs so hard she's clutching her stomach.

Pull yourself together, Trillian.

"Th–thank you for coming… for playing tonight."

Yeah, that's smooth.

Not.

"You're welcome," Jet replies.

Jet.

He's hot, too.

So is Kidd.

And Trey.

Oh, my.

Arrow, Rake, Sin, and another biker named Tracker were here, too.

Hotness overload.

Sin's old lady Faye was gorgeous and gave me her number so we could catch up sometime. Total sweetheart.

"Trillian," Xander whispers into my ear. "You better give your husband some attention right now or I'm going punch one of them in the face."

Grinning, I turn to him and kiss his mouth. "I can't believe you got them to play."

"Anything for you, Trill, you know that. Even watching you drool over men who I now want to kill."

Best. Husband. Ever.

XANDER

THREE YEARS LATER

"Fuck."

I look down at my daughter, Skye, and cringe. "Baby, that's a bad word, you shouldn't say that."

"Fuck."

I glance around, glad Trillian isn't home yet. She's still at the primary school where she works as a full-time teacher. I work as a mechanic, and I have my own garage in Channon. Today, however, I am spending the day watching Skye, who is now two. I'd said 'fuck' accidentally when I noticed that our new puppy chewed Trillian's shoes, and she heard it.

And now she's repeating it.

I am so fuckin' dead.

Whose idea was it to get a puppy when we already have a toddler, anyway?

Vixen is a German Shepherd and a beautiful dog. She is also a pain in the ass.

"Fuck!" Skye yells, looking proud of herself. Her inky blue-black curly hair is sticking up in every direction, her hazel eyes sparkling with mischief. She is absolutely perfect, and I'm going to need to invest in a baseball bat when she hits her teens.

Or a crowbar.

Oh, hell, I'll just pass out the information that her godfather is a member of the Wind Dragons MC. That will do it.

"Skye, don't say that word around Mummy, okay?" I try to barter with her.

"Okay, Daddy," she replies.

I hear the front door unlock and Trillian walk in, looking as beautiful as she was the day I met her.

"Hi, Mummy!" Skye yells, running to her. Trillian lifts her in her arms and kisses her. Then she heads straight to me, bends her head, and kisses me on my mouth.

"How was your day?" I ask her, pulling both Trillian and Skye onto my lap.

"It was good," she replies, smiling at me. "I missed you both, though. What did you two get up to?"

"Took her to the park and swimming lessons," I reply. "Then we both napped."

Trillian giggles. "Of course you did."

"I missed you," I tell her, capturing her lips in another kiss, this one open-mouthed.

I still can't get enough of her.

I never will.

"Fuck!' Skye yells.

Trillian glances down at her and then back at me. "Xander Kane!"

I shrug sheepishly.

Fuck.

Turn the page for an excerpt from *Arrow's Hell*, the second book in the *Wind Dragons MC* series by Chantal Fernando.

ARROW'S HELL

(WIND DRAGONS MC #2)

PROLOGUE

ARROW

I stare down into my Scotch, twirling the amber liquid around in the glass. The clubhouse moves around me, people talking, laughing and carrying on, but I feel like I'm frozen. Like the world is moving around me, but I'm stuck in place. I know I'm held back by my own demons, my own guilt, but I don't deserve any redemption. My neck strains as I tilt my head back, memories playing in my mind like an old movie.

Mary gathers her clothes and dresses slowly.

I take in her every move.

Everything about her is gentle.

Beautiful.

What the hell am I doing? Why do I keep her at a distance?

Faye is right—Mary is one of a kind and I shouldn't be fucking around on her. Even if she knows about it. Mary has never once tried to change me. She's taken me as I am—my many faults and all.

How many women would do the same?

"Have a safe run, Arrow," she says softly, lifting her dark hair off her back and tying it up.

"Come here," I demand softly.

She instantly complies.

She's good like that, always wanting to make me happy, but at the same time—she's not weak. She's intelligent, sharp, and knows what she wants in life.

I'm just lucky enough to be one of those things.

I want to tell her that I only want to be with her and that I'm going to do right by her.

I want to tell her I want her as my old lady.

But I don't.

"We need to talk when I get back," I say, needing time to gather the right words.

She nibbles on her bottom lip. "Is everything okay?"

"It will be," I tell her, kissing her heart-shaped lips.

It will be okay the moment I tell her how much I love her.

My eyes snap open, and I shake my head, laughing without humor.

I never did tell her that I loved her.

She was dead because of me, and she died thinking . . . What would she have been thinking? That I didn't care for her? That I should have been there to protect her? To save her? Maybe before her life faded away she wished that she'd never met me, never wasted her time on me.

She might have been right.

I lift the glass to my lips and drink, the warm liquid sliding down my throat with ease. Since getting out of prison, I've been spending some of my time at local strip clubs, and I know everyone thinks I am getting laid, but I'm not. I let them think that. The truth is, I go there to torture myself. I drink; I watch; I keep my mind busy. What I didn't do was fuck anyone. I haven't been with anyone since Mary. It has been years—five to be exact. She doesn't get to move on and live her life, so why should I? I like the fact that she is the last woman I was with. What I couldn't give to her in life I am giving her in death.

Rake walks in, a blond woman by his side. I know exactly who she is, because Rake's been bragging about her ever since the day I fuckin' met him. I've seen a picture of her, but it seems to have not done her any justice.

Anna.

Just the temptation I don't need.

Her eyes dart to me as she offers me a small smile.

I don't return it.

I peruse her body slowly, tempting myself with something I could never have.

When I feel myself harden, I know I need to get the fuck out of here. Standing up, I down the rest of my drink and place it on the table. Rake is introducing Anna to everyone, and I need to leave before it's my turn, but my feet don't seem to want to move.

What is it about this woman? I can't remember the last time I studied one so carefully. To me, they are all the same, some just come in better packaging. Maybe it is all the things Rake has told me about her over the years? I almost feel as if I know her. She's even more fuckin' beautiful up close and personal. I hear the stories about her. Everything from their childhood antics to what she's been studying in school. Rake thinks the world of her, and either he's blinded by her, or the woman truly has a heart of gold. She's apparently intelligent and sweet, but she also has a wild streak in her. And she has a fiery, tough side from what I hear.

An interesting mix for a man like me. Mary was all sweetness, but that didn't exactly work in her favor—she was just too good for me. With my lifestyle, I need a woman who can handle everything that comes with it, the good, the bad, and, most important, the ugly.

What the fuck was I thinking?

I don't need a woman right now. At least not anything long-term. I need a drink and some willing pussy, not an old lady. Anna is completely off-fuckin'-limits . I got the last woman I cared for killed. I'm not going to put anyone in that position again. Being with me isn't safe, and I don't deserve some poor woman caring about me anyway. Mary got death, but I got a sentence. Not just to prison, but to be alone. That's my penance.

The smell of a fresh vanilla scent pulls me from my thoughts. Something that doesn't help with my boner. Great, I was standing here, fuckin' daydreaming like a kid, and didn't make a getaway.

"Arrow, this is Anna," Rake says, smiling proudly. "Anna, meet Arrow."

"Nice to meet you, Arrow," she says, her plump lips curving around each word.

I nod my head. "You too."

Fuck, she's beautiful.

I look to Rake and slap him on the shoulder. "I'm going out. I'll see you later, brother."

I have no right to be attracted to Rake's sister.

So what if the moment I saw her, the world around me unfroze?

I don't deserve sweetness like that.

Rake frowns. "You can't stay a bit?" He steps closer to me so only I can hear. "I want Anna to feel welcome."

He doesn't want her to run scared, I can see it in his eyes. He's afraid she won't want anything to do with us, him, or this lifestyle.

A valid concern.

I lick my bottom lip, not wanting to hurt Rake but needing to get away right now.

He saves me. "Don't worry, you go on ahead."

"Thanks, brother," I tell him, flashing him a grateful look. I can't help myself—my eyes dart to the woman before me, to see her already watching me, a thoughtful expression on her face.

Yeah, that's not good.

"See you around, Anna," I manage to get out.

She arches a delicate brow. "You can count on it."

I leave the clubhouse feeling like something just changed, even though I know it is impossible.

Mary is six feet under, where I should be.

It should have been me. I lead this life. She was just a veterinarian who hooked up with the wrong man. A man who couldn't offer her anything other than a good fuck. Not even monogamy.

I don't need to drag anyone else down with me, what I need to do is to stay away from Anna, the first woman who's stirred any interest in me in a long time.

I get on my bike and ride away, pushing thoughts of a perky little blonde out of my head.

CHAPTER ONE
ANNA

"Do you have any plans now?" Damien asks as we walk out of the lecture.

I turn to him. "My ride will be here soon. I'm just going home. I have a lot to do."

"Oh, okay. How about this weekend?"

Damien's a nice guy, but I don't feel anything when I look at him. He is just a friend; not even that, more of an acquaintance.

"I'm going out with my best friend, Lana, this weekend," I reply, forcing a smile. I don't want to lead him on, but I don't want to hurt him either. I am horrible in these kinds of situations.

"Maybe I could take you—"

I roll my eyes as I hear the rumble of a motorcycle, stopping Damien midsentence. Sliding my phone into my bag for safekeeping, I say, "Gotta go, Damien. I'll see you tomorrow, okay?"

"'Bye, Anna."

Right on time—like clockwork.

I glance around the courtyard, then walk toward the parking lot. You would think at my age I could catch a bus home to my apartment without any drama, but that isn't the case. I don't have a car, but I'm saving up for one. However, my brother makes sure I have a lift home after class, especially if I finish in the late afternoon. I'm still not sure how I feel about it. It does feel good to have someone, my brother in particular, looking out for me, but at the same time, after doing my own thing for so long I feel a little claustrophobic.

My brother is one of my favorite people in the world, and after not having seen him for some time, I am happy to be getting to know him again. I just moved back to the city, and am finding the move easier than I had anticipated, mainly because my best friend, Lana, is here. We'd stayed in touch ever since I moved away, so I'm psyched to be so close to her now. My brother has changed, but I know that he still loves and cares about me. I'm the only family he has, after all. His overprotectiveness, however, needs to change. I know he means well and is trying to make up for lost time, but the constant escorts are beginning to drive me batshit crazy. He keeps an eye on my every move and sometimes tries to dictate them. I feel like I'm in a damn prison. I love my brother and I'm trying to make this work for the both of us, but we're both still on shaky ground, not 100 percent comfortable with each other yet. We're feeling each other out, seeing how we've both changed and how we've stayed the same.

I don't miss the curious stares from the other students on campus, but I ignore them. I can just imagine how it looks, my getting picked up every day by a different man on a motorcycle, each one of them sporting a Wind Dragons Motorcycle Club cut. Luckily for me, I'm not a young, insecure girl anymore and there's only a handful of people in the world whose opinion I actually care about. Likely they think I'm a biker groupie, or something along those lines. In reality, I'm just a twenty-five-year-old PhD student and a girl who happens to be the younger sister of a Wind Dragons MC member. If people want to judge me, that's their prerogative, and I couldn't care less.

I'm proud of my brother. He is who he is. He means well and I know he loves me. Yes, he's a biker, belonging to a motorcycle club that is well-known in these parts, but he's also a good man.

Adam's always been a good man.

He also happens to be a huge pain in my ass, a total man-whore, and overprotective to the point of stupidity. Ever since I was a little girl, he'd taken his role of big brother very seriously. It probably had to do with the fact that we didn't know who our father was, and our mother was . . . absent. That was putting it nicely—in fact, our mother was a junkie who left us to fend for ourselves ever since I could remember.

My brother also made it his business to scare off any potential dates, and that hasn't changed. If anything, it's gotten worse. It seems when most men around here find out who my brother is, they decide I'm not worth the ass kicking they'll get—but in a way it's almost like a screening test. I don't want a man who's a pussy and afraid of my brother. I want a strong man who'll tell my brother to fuck off and smile while doing it. The thought makes me grin to myself.

I wonder who my babysitter will be today.

Seeing the sexy beard and the broad, wide shoulders encased in tight black fabric, I smile widely, pleased with my escort for today. I walk straight up to his idling bike, sashaying my hips with each step.

"Good afternoon, Arrow," I say, grinning cheekily.

He narrows his eyes on me. "You gonna give me trouble today, Anna?"

Probably.

But only because he needs it. The man hardly smiles, so I find myself being more playful around him than I am around anyone else, just to get a reaction out of him.

"Anna?" he repeats, staring at me weirdly when I don't reply as I continuingto study him, lost in my own thoughts.

Fuck, but I love the way he says my name. Arrow must have a good ten years on me, but he doesn't look it. Not to me. He has a better body than most of the men my age and a beard that looks badass on him.

I do love a good beard.

You can tell that under the beard is a strong, square jaw. I wonder if he has a dimple in his chin.

He also has soulful brown eyes that you just know have seen the world at its worst, but he's still survived. He has faint crinkles on either side of his eyes, letting me know he once used to laugh a lot. His mouth is full, firm, and entirely lickable.

"I have no idea what you're talking about," I tell him with a shrug. I push my blond hair off my face and flash him an innocent look. I have the same green eyes as my brother, and while his incite lust from the opposite sex, mine don't seem to be doing the same. Arrow's face turns grumpier, if that's even possible. What the hell is he so moody about all the time? Yes, I heard he did time in jail, but most bikers do at some point, don't they? At least the ones I've heard of. Okay, I guess I shouldn't stereotype like that. But Arrow did do time, although I don't know what for. I overheard my brother talking with Tracker, another member of the MC. I've been around these bikers for a month or so now, and out of all of them, Arrow is the one who keeps both his distance *and* his guard up.

He's also the one I can't stop thinking about.

Quite a conundrum.

Well, for me anyway.

Have you ever seen someone for the first time and just *wanted* them? Something about them attracts you, like a moth to a flame, without rhyme or reason. Every time I look at Arrow I feel that pull. That want, that need. There is something about him, something that draws me to him. Sure, he is gruff and rough around the edges. He is also temperamental, broody, and usually pretty damn grumpy. He is a man of few words—the strong, silent type. The more time he is forced to spend as my babysitter, the more I've gotten him to open up. Slowly, little by little, he's started speaking to me. It is progress, but still, I know I am stupid to hope for anything more. Sure, my heart races whenever he is near, but I try to ignore that little factor as best as I can. It doesn't change anything. Arrow is my guilty pleasure, something I know I shouldn't want but want anyway. The thing is, I've seen little glimpses of him that make me believe he is more than he shows the world. I've seen him playing with Clover, the MC president's daughter, and sneaking her strawberry candy. I've seen him tickling her, her loud giggles echoing throughout the room. I then overheard him telling her that if any boy messes with her, to let him know and he would take care of it because no one hurts the princess.

She's five.

No one can tell me the man doesn't have a heart.

"Get on the bike and hold on," he demands, turning away from me. It frustrates me that he never looks at me for longer than he has to. Is he not attracted to me at all? I'm not vain, but I know that I'm not completely unfortunate in the looks department. Adam has even said I'm too beautiful for my own good, but as my brother, I guess he's a little biased.

Maybe Arrow sees me as nothing more than Adam's baby sister. Butthat doesn't explain why he always seems so eager to leave my presence. I like to think I'm easy to be around, and sometimes even a little fun.

"Where are we going?" I ask as he hands me my helmet.

"Rake wants to see you at the clubhouse," he replies distractedly.

"Then why didn't he pick me up himself?" I ask. Not that I'm complaining, since I secretly covet being around Arrow, but still.

"I was closer to campus, so it just made more sense. Now are you getting on the bike or are we gonna sit around while all these stuck-up assholes stare at us?"

I look around.

Yeah, people are still staring. If he didn't want the attention, maybe he shouldn't have worn his cut today. Who am I kidding? People would stare either way. Arrow is imposing. It is in his build, the breadth of his shoulders, the way he carries himself. The sharpness of his gaze. He just commands attention around him, and there is nothing he can do about it. He couldn't fade into the background if he tried. I slide onto the back of his bike. Wrapping my arms around his waist, I grip the leather in my hands and lean into him. He smells like leather and . . . strawberry candy? I want to ask, but before I can he starts the engine and pulls out of the lot. I hold tight, enjoying both the ride and the feel of my body pressed against his.

I'd never been on a motorcycle until I moved back here. It was a new experience, and one I found that I loved. Nothing felt more freeing, and I found myself wanting to get my own motorcycle license. If being on the back feels this way, I can only imagine how good it feels to be in front, in control of the bike.

I wonder what my brother would think about that idea.

Adam and I didn't have the best childhood growing up. Neither of us talks about it much, to each other or to anyone else—at least that's how it used to be before I left. After I turned eighteen, I moved to the other side of the country for college. That was the year Adam—or should I say Rake—joined the Wind Dragons MC. We kept in touch here and there, messages, phone calls on birthdays and holidays, but for the most part we grew apart. He was busy, I was busy, and we were too far away to be of any real use to each other. I know he's proud of me. He used to tell me every time we spoke on the phone. He was happy I was making something of myself—starting from scratch to become someone statistics prove I shouldn't be. I also know he wants the best for me, he always has, but it almost feels like he doesn't know how to act around me anymore, how to be himself. He's changed over the years, I guess being in a motorcycle club will do that, but underneath he's still my Adam. A mix of protective, sweet, and goofy and usually found with a grin on his face or a woman on his arm.

That definitely hasn't changed. My brother has always been, and will always be, a ladies' man. However, he's gotten even more protective of me than he was before I left the city, which makes no sense, because I'm not a girl anymore, I'm a grown woman. I'm his baby sister, by a year, but he's acting like I'm seventeen and trying to keep tabs on my every move. It was cute at first—but now it's getting damn annoying and he and I are in need of a good chat. I can't imagine he's any better at compromising than he was growing up, but maybe I can use my puppy-dog eyes to let him loosen the reins a little. The truth of the matter is I love being around Rake and his MC. I just don't like being controlled. I want to be there on my terms, not his. I want to be given choices and know that I'm being heard. Being around a group full of alpha males isn't easy.

I sigh against Arrow's back, enjoying the sensation of being pressed up against a man I should be glad wouldn't give me the time of day. He's dangerous, I know it and so would anyone who saw him. It is more than his physical appearance. You can almost feel the menace radiating from him, the raw power. It also doesn't take a genius to see that he has an extralarge chip on his shoulder, weighing down on his muscular build. My breasts rub against his back and I feel him tense, so I move away slightly, my fingers gripping him with more pressure than before.

The ride is quick, and Arrow's bike soon skids to a stop. I climb off, handing him back his helmet.

"Thanks, Arrow," I tell him quietly.

He grunts in response and takes the helmet from my hands, but doesn't bother to look me in the eyes.

"How's your day been?" I ask, tilting my head to the side and studying him as he gets off his bike.

He glances up at me, finally, and rubs the back of his neck. "It was okay. You gonna ask about the fuckin' weather next?"

"If I have to," I mutter, rolling my eyes. "In case you were wondering, my day was kind of awesome."

He grins then, his eyes softening on me slightly. "Good to hear, Anna, good to hear. Now get your ass inside."

He is trying to get rid of me. How predictable.

"Arrow," I say, taking advantage of his attention. "Do you think Rake will tone down the whole escort thing?"

He licks his top lip, then follows through with his teeth. I stare at his mouth, mesmerized by the action.

He clears his throat. "Don't look at me like that, Anna."

"Like what?" I ask, still staring.

"Anna," he snaps. I lift my gaze, my cheeks heating. "Go and ask Rake, but I don't think so. He just wants you safe. Bad shit has happened before, and he's going to make sure that nothing bad touches you. And I agree with him. Now get your ass inside before he calls me asking where the hell you are."

"Okay," I reply, puffing out a breath.

He steps to me and touches my cheek in an almost-there caress. Okay, this is new. He's never shown this type of affection to me before.

Our eyes lock.

I swallow hard.

He pulls away and turns his back to me. Looks like I've been dismissed.

"Nice chatting with you as always," I call out as I walk into the clubhouse. The scene before me is a familiar one. Rake is sitting there with a woman on his lap, blissfully unaware of the rest of the world. Faye, the president's wife and queen bee of the clubhouse, is talking with Tracker, another MC member and a friend of mine. Sin, the club president, is nowhere to be seen. Faye turns when she notices me, her auburn hair framing her pretty face. I nod my head at her, giving her the respect she's due as Sin's old lady.

I know Faye is a badass chick, I've heard all the stories about her. I tend to stay out of her way—we don't really interact, even though she's close with Rake, Tracker, and the rest of the guys. I think in any other situation, we'd probably really get along well. I've heard nothing but good things about her, but I still have no plans to befriend her anytime soon. I'll never admit this to anyone, but I envy her. She has all the men wrapped around her finger, but more important, they treat her like an equal. No one tells her what to do or orders her around. They listen to her and respect her. And it pisses me off that while I'm treated like a child, she can do as she pleases.

I know the men keep a close eye on me only because of Rake's commands, and I hope that will ease up when my brother realizes that I'm a woman who can take care of herself. I think he needs to figure out that he never let me down when we were younger, and he has nothing to make up for. He's a great brother, even though he can be a tad excessive when it comes to me. I know it's because of how much he cares about me, but I don't think he knows what to do about it. Or me.

Tracker walks over to me when he sees me, a smile playing on his lips, and wraps an arm around my shoulders. "Anna Bell!"

"Don't call me that," I reply, raising an eyebrow at him. Tracker is friendly, easy to get along with, drop-dead gorgeous, and completely fuckable. Shoulder-length blond hair frames a handsome face with bright blue eyes and full lips. His body is impressive, lithe and toned, and covered in tattoos. Why he's with Allie, I have no idea. I think it's one of those things—like how good girls always finish last, because the bitch definitely won when she got her paws on a man like Tracker. The first time I came to the clubhouse, he approached me and made a comment about breaking in the fresh meat. I replied with a joke about how I was harder to get than Rake, and we both found that amusing. We've kind of become friends since then. Tracker is very easy to be around, and he's a good listener. I just bonded with him from the very start.

"It's a very cute name, for a cute lady," he says, squeezing my cheeks, shaking my head left and right.

"Fuck off," I tell him with a smile, slapping away his hands.

"How was class?" he asks, pulling on a lock of my blond hair. Could he be more annoying? He treats me like the sister he never had yet didn't want, so I make sure to return the favor.

"It was okay," I reply. "Still thinking about quitting and becoming a club whore though. It seems to hold a certain appeal."

He laughs, a deep rumble. "Don't let Rake even hear you joke about that."

"What would he do? Treat me like a kid and have people escort me everywhere?" I ask, voice full of sarcasm.

"And that," he says, smirking, "is the reason you will never be a club whore."

"What?" I ask, confused.

He chuckles. "Your sharp tongue. We like the club women to be pliable and—"

"Stupid? Easy? Flexible?" I offer, waggling my eyebrows sleazily.

He laughs harder. "I was going to say accessible."

My lip twitches and I shake my head. "I can't believe we're having this conversation right now."

"It's a normal conversation for me," he adds.

"I'll bet."

"Where's that sidekick of yours?"

I narrow my eyes on him and purse my lips. "Why do you want to know?"

I sawthe way my best friend, Lana, stared at Tracker when she met him. Like he was fucking Superman or something. I caught Tracker studying her too, but didn't think much of it until now.

I know that Lana would never be someone's side chick, but Tracker has this way about him . . . I hope he just leaves her alone. Lana is smart, bookish, and doesn't have much experience with men. If Tracker shows interest in her, that's not a good thing. Allie is his woman and is so crazy—legit crazy, not just crazy in love—she'd probably claw Lana's eyes out. I don't miss the looks she gives me when I talk to Tracker, and I'm just a friend.

Of course, Allie might have to watch her back. Lana can be quiet and unassuming most of the time, but she has a serious temper on her. Trust me, I've seen it firsthand. It hardly ever comes out, but when it does, everyone is in trouble.

He shrugs like it doesn't matter to him either way. "Just making conversation. Put those claws away, Anna Bell."

Rake walks over to me like he's only just realized I've been standing here. Which he probably did.

"Hey, sis," he says as he rubs his scruffy jaw. Blond hair and green eyes the same shade as mine, my brother has an eyebrow piercing and lip ring that suit him. He's good-looking and knows it.

Yes—he's one of *those* men. He uses his good genes to his advantage and no woman is safe in his presence. I wonder when he'll settle down, and the type of woman it would take to make him do it. I'm thinking she would have to be pretty freaking phenomenal, because Rake seems to like a lot of variety and never stays with one woman long enough for me to even get to know her. Okay, that's not exactly true. Rake started acting this way only after he broke up with Bailey in high school. She was the only woman I've ever seen Rake pay any real interest to. I wonder what Bailey's up to these days.

"Hey. Why did you want me to come here?" I ask him, getting straight to the point.

He looks confused. "I thought we could hang out; I haven't seen you in a couple of days."

I blink slowly.

"Okay. Will she be joining us?" I ask, pointing to the woman who is now standing behind him wearing a pouty expression.

"Fuck, no," he replies, turning back and telling his tag-along something.

"Cut him some slack," Tracker tells me softly so no one else can hear.

My mouth drops open. "But . . . but . . ."

He grins. "I know, but he's trying."

I know he's trying; I do. He isn't used to me in his space, I'm not used to being in his space, but I I'm getting there. It is a lot to take on, being thrown headfirst into the MC lifestyle. I am adapting though, and know it means a lot to Rake that I try to fit in here.

When I see Rake walk past Faye and kiss her on the top of her head, my throat burns. How can he be so loving and affectionate with her but not his own sister?

I pretend his casual affection with her doesn't hurt.

Rake says something to Faye, and she throws back her head and laughs. "What have you done now?"

Rake grins boyishly. "Nothing . . . yet. Just need some legal advice on something. Make some time for me, woman."

Faye looks amused. "Come see me tomorrow."

My brother nods and says something to her in a low tone that I can no longer hear.

"He doesn't wanna fuck things up with you, so he's being careful," Tracker muses from beside me.

Thank you, Dr. Phil.

I sigh and lean my head on Tracker's arm. "I know he cares about me. I just wish he wasn't so . . ."

"Slutty?" Tracker adds with a wolfish grin.

I laugh, shaking my head. "No. It's almost like he's scared to be himself around me."

"I think he just wants you to be proud of him and not scare you off with his bikerish ways."

"I am proud of him," I say, cringing when he slaps the woman's ass as she leaves. "Okay, he can be a pig sometimes."

Tracker's loud laugh gets us looks from everyone in the room.

"What's so funny?" Rake asks as he walks over and moves me away from Tracker. He sends Tracker a look that says *She's my sister, asshole.*

I roll my eyes. Rake has the protective big-brother thing down pat, that's for sure. He's always looking out for me, always has.

Tracker raises his hands, proclaiming his innocence. "We're just friends, man, you know I wouldn't go there."

"And why not?" I ask him in a sweet tone. "Is there something wrong with me?"

I put my hand on my hip, cocking it to the side, and give him a look that dares him to say anything other than how I'm one of the most beautiful women he's ever seen. I try and keep my face serious, not wanting to break out in the smile that's threatening my lips.

Tracker tilts his head to the side, taking me in from top to bottom. "You kind of look like Rake if you squint your eyes, so yeah, no, thanks."

He doesn't expect the punch in the gut. "Ow! You're strong for someone so little."

Rake grunts. "Come on, Anna, stop bullying my brothers."

Tracker laughs and rubs his rock-hard stomach. Like that even hurt him.

Arrow chooses that moment to walk in, and as always, he garners my full attention. I watch as he storms into the kitchen and comes out with a bottle of Scotch in one hand, a cigarette in the other.

He plops down on the couch and starts to drink straight from the bottle.

He doesn't look up, or pay attention to anyone around him, until Faye walks over and starts to talk to him in a hushed tone. I follow behind Rake as he leads me toward a long hall, forcing myself not to look back at Arrow. We stop at a door, and he grins boyishly at me as he opens it.

"This is your room. So, you know, you always have somewhere to stay, no matter what," he says, gesturing for me to enter. The room is bare except for a stunning black leather bed.

"It's new," he explains as I turn to stare at him.

"I have my own place," I tell him, feeling confused. Growing up, we didn't really have a house. We moved around and stayed wherever we could, couch surfing or living with our mother's latest boyfriend. We didn't have a stable life, or many other things that most people took for granted. We didn't come first to our mother; the drugs did. Maybe that's why he wants me to feel as though I have a home here? That no matter what, I'll always have a place to go? A place that I will be welcome?

My heart warms at the sentiment, but it isn't necessary. I am no longer that scared little girl; I am now a woman who knows how to take care of herself.

"I know you do, but you also have a place here. With me. You will never have to worry again."

Looks like I was right.

"Rake—"

"You don't have to call me that," he says, not for the first time.

"I know, but it's weird when I'm the only one calling you Adam and no one knows who the hell I'm talking about. Although I still call you Adam in my head," I try and explain.

His laugh makes me smile. I like seeing him laugh. "It's weird having my baby sister calling me Rake."

I raise an eyebrow. "So you're nicknamed after a man who lives in an immoral way and sleeps around a lot."

I used the dictionary for that one. It says a rake is another name for a womanizer, or a libertine.

The flush that works up his neck lets me know he isn't exactly pleased to be having this conversation with me. "Maybe I just like to . . ."

He searches fruitlessly for another reason to be called Rake.

". . . get rid of leaves?" I suggest in a dry tone.

"You always were a smart-ass," he says with good nature. "Fine, I like women. Sue me. I'm the perfect example of a man you shouldn't date. Learn from it."

"Surely there are some good men around this clubhouse . . . ?" I say casually, pretending to look around.

Like Arrow.

That's what I really mean.

Rake's laughter isn't what I was expecting in response. "No one will go near you, Anna. They know you're off-limits."

"How would they know that?" I ask him suspiciously, my hackles rising.

"Because I told them," he replies, unable to keep the smugness out of his tone.

My mouth drops open. "Why would you do that?"

"Because you're my sister," he says, crossing his arms over his chest.

"Yes, but I'm not asexual," I reply dryly, walking farther into the room and sitting on my new bed.

"To me you are," I hear him mutter. "Look, Anna, now that you're back here . . . I want to be here for you, like I haven't always been in the past."

Ahh, the infamous Jacob incident.

"That wasn't your fault," I say for the hundredth time.

He ignores me.

"Do you wanna get a drink?" he asks, the conversation clearly over. "You can tell me how your week has been."

"Sure, I could use a drink."

I wonder if Arrow will share his bottle.

ABOUT THE AUTHOR

New York Times & USA Today Bestselling Author Chantal Fernando is twenty six years old and lives in Western Australia.

Her published novels include four books in the Resisting Love series – Chase, Kade, Ryder and James; the New York Times Bestselling novel Maybe This Time and its follow up, This Time Around. Her latest releases include Toxic Girl, Saxon, and a USA bestselling biker romance novel Dragon's Lair.

When not reading, writing or daydreaming she can be found enjoying life with her three sons and family.

Represented by Kimberly Brower from the Rebecca Friedman Literary Agency.

Made in the USA
Las Vegas, NV
26 January 2025

17009865R10122